A Murder Mystery Thriller

CHILL OF TRUTH

Danger and Betrayal in the
Arctic Polar Bear Capital

Tess Raynes

Table of Contents

Chapter 1: The Final Descent 4

Chapter 2: Shadows in the Snow 17

Chapter 3: Cold Comfort..29

Chapter 4: The Lodge of Secrets..43

Chapter 5: Fractured Trust..58

Chapter 6: Beneath the Ice 69

Chapter 7: Toxic Evidence..81

Chapter 8: The Calm Before..94

Chapter 9: Frozen Lies.. 109

Chapter 10: Storm of Suspicions 118

Chapter 11: Frostbitten Truths.. 131

Chapter 12: Twisted Obsession.. 146
   One Year Before – Tokyo, Japan 146
   Present Time – Churchill, Canada 147
   One Year Before – Tokyo, Japan 148
   Present Time – Churchill, Canada 150
   One Year Before – Tokyo, Japan 153

Chapter 13: Into the White 161

Chapter 1

The Final Descent

Elena Hart slumped into the seat beside the window and checked her face in the silver-plated compact she always carried. She hated flying. Scratch that; she hated traveling. It seemed like her life these days was one long commute, too many hours spent in drab, stuffy airports followed by long, uncomfortable flights, cramped hotels, endless photo shoots, senseless interviews, and press junkets.

This latest outing to Churchill, Manitoba, a remote, snow-covered town in the Canadian Arctic—a location that claimed to be the *polar bear capital of the world*—was just another in a long line of engagements she could do without, but one her agent, Max Roth, insisted upon. It wasn't that she resented the fame or the money—she'd experienced plenty of hardship growing up in Detroit, Michigan, and knew how emotionally devastating it could be to live paycheck to paycheck—but every now and again, she just wanted some time to herself, a moment to reflect on who she was and what she wanted from life. Yet, Elena knew she had to go. An entourage of eight depended on her success, and the weight of that could sometimes be overwhelming. Sometimes, she even felt her boyfriend, James Bateman, loved her for her success and not for who she was.

Recently, things had started to unravel—her relationships, her friendships, and even her own family—and she knew the only way to repair those things was to make time for them. If only she could.

"You okay, honey?"

Her boyfriend, James, slid into the seat beside her. He was holding two drinks: a whiskey soda for him and a Manhattan for her.

She smiled, took the glass, and watched as he eyed the tube of lipstick on the table.

"You know, you don't always have to be in full warpaint."

Oh, but I do, she thought, *because without it, who am I? The daughter of a factory worker, father, and office cleaner mom from the slums of the motor city? The little girl with freckles who would get bullied for wearing cheap glasses because her parents couldn't afford anything better?*

"You know how I like to be," she said. "It only takes a split second for an overeager fan to snap me with their phone camera and post the images to social media, and in an instant, there'll be a thousand trolls eager to comment on my fading looks or imperfect skin."

"Look around you, hun. There are no overeager fans on this plane. Attendance at this photo shoot is by strict invitation only. Everyone onboard has been vetted at least three times by Max and Sarah."

Sarah Locke was Elena's PR spokesperson and project manager for all her shoots. She had a healthy obsession with meticulously arranging everything, even though she could be hard to like.

"Even so," she said, sipping her drink. "I'd rather err on the side of caution."

Elena leaned back and watched as Tom Oates, her personal cameraman and documentarian, attempted to stow his bulky equipment in the compartment overhead. After three attempts at fitting his camera bag, backpack, and various tripods and camera stands into the small cupboard, he tossed his bag on the seat and turned to face her.

"You see what I have to put up with?" he said, his face the color of a ripe eggplant. "Should I really have to risk damaging my equipment because, once again, the people who arrange these things can't be bothered to check how much storage space a photographer of my experience needs?"

"Nonsense, there's plenty of room," Sarah said, emerging from the rear of the cabin, rearranging the assortment of photography and videography equipment, and sliding the backpack into the perfectly created gap.

"Do you have any idea how much a Nikon Z9 costs?" Tom asked, "or a Sachtler Flowtech?"

"No, actually I don't," Sarah said, her blond hair tied back in a ponytail, a wry smile kissing her lips, "so why don't you educate me?"

Tom's eyes flitted from Sarah to Elena and back again, his mouth opening and closing like a floundering salmon. "A lot," he said. "Far too much for someone like you to be slamming it into an overhead locker so carelessly."

"It's good to see you're in such a good mood, Tom," Sarah replied. "This trip should be fun."

Elena shook her head. "Why don't we all just sit back and enjoy the flight? I hear Churchill is a beautiful town."

Tom eyed Sarah, shot a cautious glance at Elena, and conceded ground, dropping heavily into his chair, retrieving a dog-eared paperback from his jacket pocket, and thumbing the pages furiously.

From behind the curtain, a petite young woman with dark eyes and shoulder-length hazel hair appeared. Her name was Lily Craven, and she was Elena's friend and personal makeup artist.

Lily spotted James and shot him a warm smile before turning her attention to Elena. "How you doing?" she asked.

"I'm fine," Elena replied, reaching out and grabbing the woman's hand. "I asked Max to find out where you were. Is everything okay?"

"I've had one of those mornings. Sorry. I'd planned to be here an hour ago. Mom wasn't feeling so good, so I had to fix her meds, and then the traffic on the freeway was insane."

"You poor thing. Is she okay?"

"Oh, you know?" Lily replied. "She knows the score, and she's accepted it. We're just living day by day, accepting what we have."

Elena couldn't help but feel sad for her friend. She also felt ashamed. She'd meant to check in on Sally Craven, Lily's mother, but she'd been so busy she'd simply forgotten. She had no excuses. She'd been friends with her makeup artist since they were both starting out in the industry, and she'd spent many evenings at the home Lily shared with her mother, eating pasta, drinking wine, and telling funny stories. Sally had always been good to her, even before she'd known where her life was headed. She'd received her terminal cancer diagnosis over six months ago, but Elena had yet to visit.

"I'd understand if you wanted to stay behind to care for her," she said, trying in some way to atone for how crap a friend she was. "I'm sure Sarah could find somebody capable of flying out to Churchill to take your place."

"Are you kidding me," Lily said, sliding into the chair opposite. "And let somebody else take care of your makeup? No way. Your face is mine, Elena Hart, and I'm not about to let some fresh-faced intern take it away from me."

Elena laughed. Lily had always had the ability to do that to her, to switch her emotions from sad to happy in a split second. She guessed that was why they'd grown so close. Lily was always by her side, following her around like a shadow. Sometimes, it could feel a little claustrophobic, a little too stifling.

James would get frustrated that they rarely had a moment together without Lily calling or tapping on the door, but as Elena explained to him, the modeling industry could isolate people and make them feel like they had no one to turn to. Lily was the antidote for that. She'd been there when Elena needed her the most, even at the expense of her own career. Elena would never forget that.

"Morning people," Max Roth hollered as he arrived in the cabin, a mobile phone tucked in the crook of his neck. He wore tailored, ash-gray pants, a cotton jacket the color of olives, and a crisp, white shirt. "You ready for this short hop to Narnia?"

"As ready as we'll ever be," Tom replied, still thumbing through his dime-store crime novel.

"And how's my number one client?" Max asked, turning to Elena. "You ready to make love to the camera?"

Max had a way of saying inappropriate things and feigning innocence. "I think I'll stick to my usual routine if you don't mind," Elena replied.

"As it's been turning water into wine for these past few years, I don't mind at all, Elena, my angel," he replied, moving aside as a younger, rigid-looking man appeared. He moved to the front of the plane and placed his holster onto the seat closest to the cockpit. "You've met Officer Rodriguez, I assume?"

The tall man with broad shoulders, a thick neck, and a slim waist turned to face them. He glanced at Lily, eyed James, and then turned his attention to Elena, thrusting out a hand. "It's a pleasure to meet you, Ms. Hart," he said, his voice gruff but well-clipped. "Michael Rodriguez. I'm the Air Marshal assigned to ensure you're looked after during this trip."

"It's a pleasure to meet you, Air Marshal Rodriguez," she replied, taking his hand. "I feel safer knowing you're here with us."

He slipped his fingers around her palm and gripped her a little tighter than she felt comfortable with. "I have to tell you, Ms. Hart, I'm a big fan. I've been following you since that first shoot you did for Vanity Fair."

"That's so nice of you to say. It always warms my heart when I meet people who've been with me since the beginning."

"Oh, I've been with you since the very beginning," he replied, his hand still locked around hers, his dark eyes unblinking. "And every day since. Every single step of the way."

She smiled, but in truth, his attention was starting to unsettle her. She looked down at her hand. "Maybe you could—"

"Oh, I'm so sorry," he said, the color rising to his cheeks. "I guess my inner fan got the better of me there. Don't worry, I'm not a crazy."

"Don't be silly. It's fine. I just need my hand for other things."

"Of course you do," he said, hastily retreating to his seat. "But don't worry, Ms. Hart. Your safety is my priority."

Elena eyed Sarah, who offered her a curt shrug. "What can I say? He comes highly recommended," she whispered.

"Who by?" James replied. "Arkham Asylum?"

"Oh, don't be so cold," Elena said. "He was just trying to be kind. Just be thankful we have somebody looking out for us on this trip. We're not always afforded such a luxury." She thought of her modeling assignment in Chile when a group of fans managed to get on board the bus that was transporting her from Bahia Inglesa to Zapallar. The scene had become so out of control that the local police had to get involved. Although the fans obviously just wanted autographs, the whole thing had been way too close for comfort.

The last two passengers to board the plane arrived a few moments later: a rugged-looking man in his late forties called Leonard—or Leo—Bryant and Elena's personal stylist, Samantha Mitchel, a young woman who Elena had learned was all business and as blunt as an old pencil. The pair of them looked flustered as if they had been caught doing something they shouldn't, which Elena suspected was more like the truth. She'd heard the rumors like everybody else, but she didn't care. She'd hardly been a saint in the past.

"Sorry, Elena," Samantha said. "I bumped into Leo in the coffee shop at the terminal. We're old friends, and, er—"

"We caught up on old times," Leo replied, looking at Samantha as if she was some sort of local delicacy. Elena didn't know Leo very well, but she knew his reputation. He was a laid-back, artsy type who dressed in casual clothing, talked like a man half his forty-six years of age, and spent far too much time hanging around the opposite sex. The smell wafting along the aisle suggested he and Samantha had been drinking something a little stronger than coffee.

Tom turned in his seat, set down his paperback, and shot Leo a frustrated glare. "I hope you'll be more punctual when we actually have to set up the equipment and get to work."

"Oh, don't worry, Tom," Leo replied, flapping a hand. "Have I ever let you down before?"

Tom and Leo had worked in the industry for years, often bidding against each other for some of the more lucrative shoots. Tom looked down on his more relaxed colleague's laissez-faire approach, often suggesting out loud that it belied a distinct lack of professionalism.

"There's a first time for everything," he said with more than a hint of contempt.

Leo and Samantha smirked at each other before retiring to the rear of the plane just as the captain made an appearance from the cockpit.

"Excellent, I can see everybody's now on board," he said while checking his watch. "And in the nick of time, too. Ms. Hart, it's a pleasure to have someone of your renowned fame on my aircraft, and to all of you, welcome onboard this Gulfstream G650, a plane I have had the pleasure of being captain of for the past three years. My name is Captain Jeremy Watts, and this is my co-pilot, Lieutenant Jason Meyer. Together, we will be flying you from Chicago, O'Hare, to the polar bear capital of the world. The weather forecast is pretty good, meaning we should have a smooth trip, ensuring we get you to your destination in a little over three hours. That should mean I have you down and on the tarmac by around 12:15 p.m., giving y'all plenty of time to get to the picturesque town of Churchill before lunch. In the meantime, the lovely Zoe will be attending to your needs, serving you a delicious breakfast that I've had the pleasure of consuming many times, and making sure you have everything you could possibly want. Now, before we go back behind that closed door, do any of you have any questions?"

"Yeah, where can I get myself a Cuba Libre on the rocks," Max chimed in, grinning like a kid on a school trip.

"That would be me," the flight attendant said, emerging from the kitchen area with a tray full of glasses and snacks. "Let me just hand these out, and then I'll make you that cocktail, sir."

With the captain and his co-pilot now safely in position, Elena took a moment to think about what this shoot meant for her. She'd posed plenty of times in picturesque surroundings before, but none quite as stark and remote as the little town on the west coast of the Hudson Bay. The shots were for Cosmopolitan magazine, which had interviewed her a few weeks back. The article was going to be a piece on how Elena had hustled her way from the slums of her home city, tending bars and working restaurants while she figured out what she wanted to do, eventually being spotted in the street by a man named Hank Rothchild, one of the chief scouts for Stargazer modeling agency, and bagging a few photo shoots with companies whose ethical standards were less than exemplary before being selected for a Stella McCartney catwalk at New York Fashion Week. After that, her career took off at an extraordinary rate, one which had yet to slow down. If anything, it was accelerating. The working headline for the piece was *Elena Hart, The Girl Who Emerged From The Cold*, hence the choice of Churchill, Manitoba. Max firmly believed the article would propel her to even more fame and global recognition, placing her in the hands of millions of Americans who were yet to truly appreciate her beauty. Elena thought the whole thing was a little too self-serving and an exercise in narcissism. In fact, she was more than a little embarrassed by the whole thing. However, Max, for all his faults—of which there were many—had proven himself to be an astute businessman, and he'd steered her career through some choppy waters since their first encounter in a cocktail bar in Midtown, Detroit, gaining her international acclaim and a bank balance that made her eyes water. After her initial reluctance and a series of long chats with James and Lily, she'd accepted the interview.

What didn't help was that ever since taking a particularly turbulent flight to Europe, she'd dreaded ever boarding an airplane again. When Max told her the only way to get to Churchill was by either taking a chartered flight and enduring at least two stopovers or chartering a private jet, she'd taken the latter option without a second's hesitation. Now she wished they'd just hired an RV and taken a road trip, but you can't get to Churchill by land, only by air.

"Here," James said, handing her two Valiums. "These will help calm your nerves."

He was trying to be gentlemanly, but she knew he was hardly what he seemed. Sure, their relationship had been passionate and fun, but both of them were afflicted with the kind of emotional immaturity often found in busy professionals. While James did a good job of feigning attentiveness and loyalty, she also knew she couldn't trust him. She'd come to that conclusion a few months ago when she'd found messages on his phone that implied something else was going on, something that deep down she'd known would come eventually. She'd been considering her options ever since.

Regardless, she swallowed the pills, relishing the comfort of them as they slipped down her throat. Pretty soon, she would be in a state of complete peace, a million miles away from the pressures of Cosmopolitan magazine and the fear of the paparazzi.

There was the sound of the plane roaring into life as the captain steered them toward the runway and the repetitive clicks of seat belts locking into place as Lily leaned across the table and took Elena's hand in hers. James joined in, and for a moment, they were the perfect triangle.

"This is it," Lily said to both of them. "Hold tight because things are about to change for the better."

Elena forced a smile, trying to hide the hard knot she felt in her stomach. Better sounded good. Better sounded fantastic. She only hoped it was as good as it seemed.

***

Zoe Fields stood in the kitchen of the Gulfstream G650 and watched as the multitude of characters aboard the plane jostled for attention. It was like watching one of those reality TV shows, the ones where contestants were selected because of their extreme character traits rather than their suitability for the activity, ensuring that the producers got the kind of TV gold that favored ratings rather than acceptable behavior.

She knew Elena Hart. Of course, she did. Any woman with a pulse who paid attention to the media knew of the woman from Detroit with stunning looks, elegant grace, and an ever-changing love life. The tabloids focused on the man on her arm almost as much as they focused on her career, weaving outrageous tales of midnight liaisons, illicit hookups with Hollywood actors, and secret phone calls.

When she'd learned she'd be looking after Elena and her entourage, she was so excited. She'd wanted to tell everyone she knew, especially her best friend, Tabitha, but then the fast-talking lady with the long blond hair, Sarah Locke, had arrived at her door with a Non-Disclosure Agreement and demanded that she sign it or lose the assignment. After that, she'd had to bite her lip every time she saw anybody because the first thing she wanted to tell them about was the fact she'd be spending three hours of up close and personal time with one of the most well-known people on the planet.

What she hadn't counted on was the soap opera of craziness that she'd had to deal with for the past couple of hours.

Firstly, there was the agent, Max, the kind of guy who made her skin crawl. He wasn't a misogynist as such, but he certainly flirted with the idea. His first act was to demand a Cuba Libre while she was arranging champagne for the other passengers. That in itself was okay—she'd dealt with worse—but then he kept asking her if she was single or if she had a significant other. The guy was old enough to be her father or at least a much older brother. She'd stood him down coolly, of course—she'd been trained to disarm members of the opposite sex in a tactful but direct way—but then he'd decided he wanted something to eat, followed by some snacks, followed by another drink. He was the kind of attention-demanding weirdo she'd had to put up with at college, except he was much older and had a ton more money.

Secondly, there was the guy with the paperback and all the cameras—Tom. His clothes were creased, his hair unruly, and he had the look of someone who felt constant displeasure at his surroundings and with those around him. She'd brought him his breakfast—a plate of pancakes and crispy bacon—but he'd practically thrown it back at her, asking her whether she was trying to "give him a heart attack." He'd barely touched his coffee or his champagne and had spent the past two hours huffing at anybody that got within three feet of him and shooting Elena and her team the kind of looks most people reserved for their worst enemies.

The Air Marshal, Mike Rodriguez, was the most polite man on the flight, thanking her profusely whenever she took something to him, eating his food politely and without fuss, and rolling his eyes at her whenever any of the other passengers did something annoying. She liked him. He had the air of somebody who knew his place in the world, respected it, and looked after those around him. She felt safe with him on board.

Elena's partner, James, was a little aloof but otherwise polite. He was dressed in the kind of clothes and accessories only the extremely wealthy could afford—a Gucci jacket, Armani pants, and a gleaming Rolex—and he smelled of expensive, heady cologne. He looked at home in his environment, relishing every detail, every complementary drink, hot face towel, and tasty delicacy. He talked to Zoe in a way that the casual observer might mistake for the banter of old friends. If she were younger and a little more naive, she might have thought him charming, but she'd met people like James Bateman before, and she knew that sincerity was not a currency he traded in. He was a little too oily, a little too slick. When he'd brushed past her to go the men's room, she'd had to suppress the urgent need to go and wash her hands.

Elena's make-up artist and friend, Lily Craven, was much more of a people person, professional on the outside but a lot softer and empathetic beneath her hard exterior. She'd even made time to get up from her seat and chat with her, asking questions about her life outside of work, her family, and her education and generally making her feel like she cared. She seemed like the odd one out amongst all the wealth, inflated egos, and barely concealed bitterness. She could see why Elena kept Lily by her side. She was an island of normality in a sea of craziness.

By contrast, Elena's PR spokesperson, Sarah Locke, was a tightly wound ball of energy, constantly on the move, never relaxing or allowing herself a moment of quiet contemplation. She never touched any of the alcohol and only picked at the gluten-free salad she'd ordered before take off. She was constantly on Zoe, ensuring that she was checking on each of the passengers, particularly those she saw as more important—namely Max, James, and Elena herself. She was an attractive woman, smartly dressed with discreet but immaculate makeup, a well-toned body, and sharp intellect—but something about her told Zoe that she wasn't entirely happy with where she'd ended up in life. Maybe it was the casual glances at Elena or the way she kept checking herself in the mirror, but Zoe doubted she was quite as confident or poised as she made herself out to be.

That left the two latecomers at the rear of the plane—the photographer, Leo Bryant, and Elena's stylist, Samantha Mitchell. They'd taken seats on either side of the aisle when they'd boarded and had been locked in conversation ever since. It was clear to Zoe that the photographer was far more attracted to the elegant stylist than she was to him, but it didn't stop him from flirting outrageously and nudging her impishly whenever Zoe appeared. Nevertheless, Zoe liked him. He wasn't bothered at all by the luxury afforded to him by his presence with the group and didn't care what he did or said. Similarly, Samantha was locked into her work and wasn't paying attention to what happened further up the cabin, and even though she entertained Leo's outlandish behavior, it was clear she would never let it undermine her role in the team. Their little whispers and furtive glances were odd, but Zoe guessed they were a symptom of a prior history they thought better to keep under wraps than publicize to the whole group.

That left Elena, the star of the show, and the reason why they were all there. Zoe knew from her pre-briefing with the captain that the glamorous model was not a happy flyer, and she'd spotted James slipping her a couple of Valium before takeoff. It hadn't taken long for the sedatives to kick in, and less than thirty minutes after they were in the air, Elena's eye mask was on, and she'd slipped off. Zoe admired her for that. Others in her position would have taken full advantage of the lavish jet and the onboard entertainment, but Elena seemed completely detached from it, as if it was all so unreal to her.

James had since decamped to the seating area in the rear cabin, accompanied by Max, Lily, and Sarah. Tom, on the other hand, had remained seated, choosing to ignore everybody else and diligently burying himself in his book. Air Marshal Rodriguez, by contrast, just sat there with his arms folded

"Excuse me, sir," Zoe asked Tom, wheeling a cart full of hot drinks and pastries. "Can I offer you a tea or a coffee? A water, perhaps?"

Tom looked up from his book. "I'm fine, thank you," he said, gesturing toward the rear of the plane. "I'm just trying to enjoy the peace and quiet before I have to deal with those imbeciles again."

She nodded politely and moved on, not wanting to poke the bear any more than she already had.

She glanced at the next cabin. James was seated next to Lily, sharing a private joke with her, which she seemed to find unfunny; Sarah was anxiously rummaging through her bag, and Max was knocking back yet another rum and coke. Behind them, Leo was leaning over Samantha and pointing toward something on her laptop screen. All of them were lost in their own worlds, and not one of them seemed concerned about whether the one person who made it all possible was okay.

Zoe went to Elena and peered down at her. She looked so peaceful as if nothing in the world could ever trouble her, but she suspected that was a million miles from the truth. Her mother always said she had a knack for reading people, and her read of Elena Hart was that she was a woman out of place in a world she didn't truly understand and never really wanted. That made Zoe sad.

She stooped over Elena to collect her half-consumed Manhattan and untouched eggs when Elena's head slumped to one side, and her mask slipped sideways. The movement revealed one completely open eye, the pupil bloodshot and unseeing. Elena's hand fell limply from her lap and brushed Zoe's arm, causing the flight attendant to cry out and jump backward.

"What the heck?" Tom said, rising from his seat. "Can't I get just a moment of peace around here?"

Zoe couldn't take her eyes off that one unblinking eye and the pale, lifeless skin of Elena's upturned palm.

"What's going on?" James asked, leaning across her to see his girlfriend reclining at an unnatural angle. "Elena, honey, are you okay?"

Air Marshal Rodriguez was the next to arrive, placing a hand on Elena's wrist and checking his watch. "This is impossible," he said. "I've been with her this whole time."

James pushed him aside and removed Elena's eye mask, revealing the other unmoving eye. It was open, just like the other, staring at a point in the distance that nobody else would ever see.

"What do you mean this is impossible?" James asked, grabbing the Air Marshal by the shoulders. "Why is she sitting there like that?"

Rodriguez's expression darkened as he turned to Zoe. "I need access to the airplane's communication system," he said. "We need to inform the authorities in Churchill."

"I...I don't understand," Zoe replied, struggling to take everything in. "What authorities? What do you need to tell them?"

"Mr. Bateman, Miss Fields," the Air Marshal said, addressing each of them as Elena's best friend appeared in the aisle. "I'm afraid it isn't good news."

The whole group was there now, each of them looking down on their boss's motionless body.

"I'm afraid Elena Hart is dead."

Chapter 2

Shadows in the Snow

Detective Ethan Steele grabbed a hot cup of coffee from the dispenser and watched as a Boeing 747 took to the skies. He always marveled at how a huge lump of steel, aluminum, and iron, filled with hundreds of people and many more items of luggage and equipment, managed to somehow take off and climb to 35,000 feet above sea level, traveling thousands of miles around the globe before landing without any problems. There were so many thousands of things that could go wrong, but most of the time, they didn't. He'd never been afraid of flying, but that didn't mean he understood the magic. Perhaps that's why he wasn't scared, because in his experience, once you knew the trick, you knew exactly what the frailties were, and that was more terrifying than ignorance.

Churchill Airport wasn't as big as some of the larger international hubs, but it was still able to serve as a diversion landing strip for some of the major airlines in case of snow storms or technical glitches. The town's location on the edge of Hudson Bay, right there on the cusp of the Arctic Circle, meant that it had its fair share of strong winds, heavy clouds, and treacherous ice, and the local authorities always dealt with these issues in the same matter of fact way, as if they were the most normal thing in the world.

"Did you get that for me?" Dr. Emily Carter said, taking the steaming Styrofoam cup and sipping the hot liquid. "Hey, thanks. Appreciate it."

"Actually, that was mine," Ethan replied, retrieving his wallet from his pocket and ordering another. "But go ahead, help yourself."

"I think you'll find I just did."

"Yeah, I did notice."

"So what do we have?" the petite doctor with long auburn hair and sharp brown eyes asked, heading toward the window and watching overhead as thick, gray clouds rolled in.

"Oh, you know, the usual. World famous supermodel boards a plane in Chicago, and then halfway through the journey is found lifeless in her seat."

Emily puffed out her cheeks. "Cause of death?"

"The Air Marshal didn't know. He sounded pretty shocked by the whole thing."

"I'm not surprised."

"Exactly?"

"How many onboard?"

Ethan held up his fingers and hand and counted. "Including the crew, I'd say around fourteen."

"Wow, and nobody saw a thing?"

"Apparently not. The first they realized something was wrong was when the flight attendant cleared the victim's table."

"That's pretty impressive."

"For the supermodel or for the killer?"

"Assuming there was a killer. This could have been natural causes, right? How old was she?"

"Twenty-eight."

"Okay, so a natural death would be unusual."

"Right. Although you and I both know these things are never simple."

Ethan had been working with Dr. Emily Carter on cases across Canada for a couple of years now, and they had forged the kind of friendship that meant cutting sarcasm and friendly jibes were par for the course. He wouldn't have it any other way. Working with Emily was much better than working with some of the stuffier medical professionals he'd had the distinct displeasure of being associated with since he became a detective over five years ago. She was funny in an understated way, sharp as a surgeon's knife, and meticulous to a fault, even though sometimes her burning need to dot every 'i' and cross every 't' drove him crazy.

Emily came from a long line of doctors and scientists. Her grandfather had worked for one of Canada's leading medical companies in the research and development department, and her mother and father both worked in a family practice, dealing with everything from broken toes to chronic heart disease. Emily, on the other hand, had chosen to be a doctor of pathology and forensic science and had graduated from the University of Toronto at the top of her class. Not content at stopping there, she'd also convinced her superiors to allow her to undertake extensive criminal justice training alongside specialist training in firearms, investigative techniques, and major case management. Emily Carter was a force to be reckoned with and one that Ethan valued immensely.

"This could be them now," Ethan said, watching as the Gulfstream approached.

"Woah, a private jet," Emily exclaimed. "They've obviously spared no expense."

"I don't think Elena Hart needs to worry about the cost of a private jet."

Emily's head snapped toward him. "Wait, did you say Elena Hart?"

"Didn't I mention her name before?"

"No. You didn't."

He smirked, playing a game he knew was dangerous.

"You mean Elena Hart as in *the* Elena Hart," Emily continued. "The Elena Hart who attended the Met Gala with Gigi Hadid? The Elena Hart who sang with Jimmy Fallon on the Tonight Show? The Elena Hart who danced with the freaking President of the United States?"

He cocked a finger in her direction. "That's the one."

Emily dropped onto a seat. "Holy cow."

Ethan plucked the empty coffee cup from her hands and tossed it in the trash. "If I were you, I'd make sure the people at home know you might be away for a while because the boss wants this case cracked as soon as possible, which can only mean one thing."

"Everybody on that plane has to be kept in one place, at least until we know whether we have a murder on our hands."

Ethan watched as the Gulfstream touched down, silently wondering what the hell had happened up there, somewhere between Chicago and the Hudson Bay.

"Exactly," he growled. "We keep them isolated, and we keep them guessing because one thing's for certain. If Elena Hart was murdered, at least one of the people on that airplane was responsible."

***

Ethan called his office and made the arrangements. The Churchill Police Department had a location by the river that they used for training purposes. It was a remote lodge, accessed by a single dirt track, and it was big enough to house everybody on the plane with an outbuilding that he thought could double as a makeshift morgue. Emily wanted the body to be examined as soon as possible, and she wanted to carry out the autopsy herself. The pair of them knew that as soon as the news of Elena Hart's death was leaked to the press, they would be confronted by a deluge of journalists and photographers, all wanting access to the passengers, the detective in charge of the case, and the money shot of Elena Hart's lifeless corpse. There was no way they could risk bringing anyone in on the investigation without a long and intense series of background checks, and they didn't have time for that—not if they wanted to stand any chance of keeping things under wraps and getting to the real truth sometime this decade.

"You good with this?" he asked Emily as they waited for the Gulfstream to make its way to the gate.

"You mean being holed up with you and a bunch of potential killers for the next few days while I try to figure out what one of the most famous supermodels in the world died from? Yeah, sure. No problem."

"Good, because with this being such a high-profile case, things are likely to get a little intense. I don't wanna kid you into thinking this is going to be easy, Em."

"They never are."

"True, but this one—"

"I think I can handle it, Ethan. Can you?"

He bit his bottom lip. It wasn't the weekend he was planning, that was for sure, but this was his job. Ever since Rebecca's death and the farce of an investigation that followed, he'd made it his life's goal to make sure others didn't suffer the same fate. He'd been a mess for a long time after that, not knowing who he could trust or who he could talk to. Somewhere out there, the person who had torn his life apart was still free, living an existence that had been robbed from his fiancée. That was not okay. People had to be held to account for their actions, no matter how powerful or influential they were.

The officer at the gate signaled for them to proceed as the ground crew piloted the staircase to the vehicle's door.

"Here we go, "Emily said. "Let's go meet our suspects."

***

"Detective Steele," Ethan said, holding up his badge to the Air Marshal, "and this is Dr. Emily Carter. She'll be the leading pathologist on this case."

The guy with the square jaw and heavy brow eyed Ethan and then glanced at Emily. Ethan had encountered this type of reaction before. The Air Marshal was obviously ex-military. The same could not be said of either he or Emily. That made them inferior in the soldier's eyes, civilians in wolf's clothing.

"Air Marshal Michael Rodriguez," he said eventually.

"It's a pleasure to meet you. I'll be needing to speak with you a little later, but for now, can you take us to the victim's body?"

"Of course. I instructed the other passengers to stay in the rear cabin so as not to disturb any evidence. I also remained in the opposite aisle and left everything exactly as it was the moment we realized Elena was no longer with us."

Ethan thought it a strange turn of phrase, as if the supermodel had simply got up and exited the plane.

The cabin wasn't large, and Ethan spotted Elena's unmoving body immediately. There was no doubt that she was no longer in the land of the living. The way her eyes were staring dead ahead and her skin had taken on the milky pallor of the deceased, left him in no doubt. He'd seen victims like this several times, people who'd been living and breathing one moment, no doubt looking forward to whatever they had planned that day, and then, in an instant, the lights went out. Elena Hart had been a hugely successful woman with a bright future ahead of her, and now everything she had worked for, all the hours of sweat and toil, the interviews, the catwalks, the endless photo shoots, had been wiped out, erased for all eternity.

The first thing he noticed was the unnatural tilt of her head and the headrest cover which was unusually twisted. He shot Emily a glance. She had spotted it, too.

"We'll need to get the body into a lab environment as soon as possible," she said, checking for a pulse, even though they both knew she'd find nothing. "There are no obvious signs of trauma, but in my experience, it's the things you don't see that shine the brightest light on the truth."

"Of course," the Air Marshal replied. "I'll confess, I don't know the facilities available to the Churchill PD at all. I assume you have a place in mind?"

Before Emily could answer, a woman's face poked through the curtain. She had a sharp nose, high cheekbones, and hazel hair. Her eyes were red-rimmed, her face blotchy. She looked at Emily.

"Are you the doctor? Can you help her? Please tell me you can."

"Ma'am, I'm going to have to ask you to go back to the next cabin and await further instructions," Ethan said, ushering her away from the curtain just as another face appeared. This one he recognized. He'd seen him on the cover of Hello magazine alongside his newly deceased partner.

"I hope you're going to catch the bastard who did this," James hissed, his voice wavering.

"We don't know yet whether there was any foul play, sir," Emily replied. "We'll need the time to do a thorough investigation. In the meantime—"

"I don't care what it takes or how much it costs. Somebody on this plane did this, and I want to know who." He spun to the rear of the cabin dramatically, gesturing to the other passengers. "I mean it. There'll be no hiding place, nowhere to run. I will find you."

Ethan ushered him to a seat as the captain emerged from the cockpit. After introducing his co-pilot, he asked Ethan whether there was anything he needed.

"Well, actually, yes, there is," Ethan said, turning to the others. "Whatever plans you had, I suggest you cancel them because until we get to the bottom of this, you're all coming with us."

***

Ethan arranged for a bus to take the passengers and the body to the remote lodge, figuring the best way to keep the investigation as low-key as possible was to move the whole group swiftly and efficiently without drawing attention to themselves.

They moved through the one-building terminal, Ethan at the front and Emily bringing up the rear with the Air Marshal beside her, both trying to ensure that nobody strayed. Beside them, two medical orderlies pushed the gurney carrying Elena Hart's corpse, which they'd sealed inside a body bag. A man in a polar bear suit came toward them, his arms outstretched in greeting, but Emily quickly intercepted him, moving him aside before he had time to realize what was going on.

The disconsolate passengers shuffled along reluctantly, none of them particularly happy at the thought of being cooped up together while the detectives interrogated them.

"This is in breach of our civil rights," Tom, the scruffy-looking photographer, said, jabbing a finger in Emily's direction. "You have no right to contain us like this. I have a business to run, you know? And I assume I won't be getting paid for this job now that the person I was supposed to be photographing is no longer with us?"

Ethan had been shocked at the brutality of the comment but used every ounce of his composure to placate the guy's protests. "All we're doing here, Mr. Oates, is trying to ascertain all the facts as swiftly as possible, and given that you're all a long way from home, the best way to do that is to keep all the potential witnesses together. The quicker you all cooperate with us, the faster we'll get to the bottom of what happened to Ms. Hart, and then we can let you all leave."

"So, are we under arrest?"

"Nobody is under arrest here, and nobody is being charged. Not yet."

"But it could happen?"

"It's a possibility."

That comment seemed to stun the whole party into silence. It was the first time anybody had even hinted at the possibility of a criminal conviction.

"We'll do whatever you need," the blond woman, Sarah, said, looking down at the body on the gurney. "Of course, we want to find out what happened. We all do. For Elena's sake."

There were muted murmurings among the rest of the group, but the project manager's interjection seemed to have quietened any more complaints, at least for the time being.

Ethan turned to his partner and signaled toward the door as they approached the exit to the parking lot. The bus was waiting just outside, which meant there would be less than half a minute of exposure before everybody on the plane was out in the open. If they were quick, they wouldn't be spotted.

A maintenance team obscured the window, so Ethan didn't see the group of photographers and the hoard of onlookers until it was too late. They emerged into the open and were immediately surrounded by dozens of eager fans and would-be journalists yelling furious questions.

"Can you confirm what happened on the plane?"

"Is that Elena Hart's body?"

"Have you found the murderer yet?"

"Do you believe she killed herself?"

Ethan pushed through the crowd, yelling at anybody who stood in his way, shoving people back as he ushered the flustered members of the entourage onto the bus. He helped the medical team wheel the gurney onto the rear storage area of the vehicle before climbing on board.

"Stand back!" Emily hollered, holding out her badge and gesturing for the crowd to make way. "If you get in the way of these people, you will be arrested for obstructing a police investigation."

"So you are investigating?" somebody yelled. "Can we take that to mean it's all true and that the body on the gurney is that of supermodel Elena Hart?"

"I didn't say that," Emily said before hauling herself onto the bus. "I didn't say that," she repeated to Ethan as the door closed.

"I know, and it doesn't matter. What does matter is how all these people found out about Elena's death."

"I think you might want to see this," the stylist, Samantha, said, holding out her phone. "It just came through. Looks like it was posted an hour ago."

Ethan stared at the screen, wondering what the hell he was looking at. It was a Twitter social media feed with just three sentences of text.

Just learned some sad news. Our very famous passenger (recently posed for GQ magazine - hint, hint) didn't make it to the other side. May be offline for a while.'

"Where did this come from?" Emily asked, re-reading the message.

"Look at the top," Samantha replied.

Ethan's eyes followed the stylists fingernail that pointed toward the top of the page. What he saw made his blood boil. The Twitter feed profile was J_Meyer1996, a.k.a. Jason Meyer, the airplane's co-pilot.

"I didn't think it would be a problem," the co-pilot said, looking over Ethan's shoulder as he read the message. He looked decidedly sheepish and more than a little flustered.

"So when I said this needed to be kept under wraps, you thought putting an announcement on one of the world's largest social media feeds was the right thing to do?"

"I was just letting my followers know that I wouldn't be able to answer their messages right away."

"It's people like you that make our jobs almost impossible," Ethan hissed, passing the phone back before turning to the window. The captain glared at his much younger colleague, shaking his head in disappointment.

The crowd outside had grown to more than forty people, all of whom were clamoring to get a shot inside the vehicle. Keeping this thing quiet was now completely impossible—they'd all seen the post, and it was serving to feed their insatiable appetite for soundbites and photo opportunities. It meant they were going to have to make the best out of a bad situation with what little resources they had.

"Just to make it clear," he said to the group. "From this point on, you don't post anything about our investigation, you don't tell anybody anything, you don't let your friends and family know where you are, you don't say anything, you hear? I want complete secrecy until we conclude our interviews. Do you all understand that?"

A few heads bobbed up and down; others just glared accusingly at the now red-faced co-pilot.

"Okay, that's good. What's done is done, so the only thing we can do is try to contain it."

"And how do we do that?" the captain asked, looking visibly shaken.

"By getting out of here as soon as possible."

***

The journey to the police training lodge was a little longer than expected as they passed through a desolate, snow-covered landscape. On route, they passed the Hudson Bay, which had already started to freeze. A cream-colored polar bear was curled up on the shore by the water, sleeping. The wind slammed into the side of the bus repeatedly as the sky overhead grew darker with billowing, gray clouds. The few homes they passed on the way contained snowmobiles or ATVs in the driveway, and Ethan was struck by the lack of people on the streets or in the yards.

The landscape, however, was something else. Rocky hills jutted from the horizon to the southwest, the snow-capped trees of the boreal forest lay to the south, and the stark, ice-covered tundra planes stretched off into the distance. Ethan began to wonder what they would do if the bus broke down or a snowstorm buried the road. How would the emergency services even get to them? He knew that the only way in and out of Churchill, other than by airplane, was via a single railroad track, making the town about as remote as a shopping mall on the moon, but without the designer clothing and burger joints.

"Is this place much further," Emily asked, "I'm starting to feel like we're heading out to visit Santa."

"Less than a mile," Ethan replied. "And anyway, I thought you liked Christmas."

"I like the ham, the eggnog, and the giving of gifts. I never said I wanted to visit."

"Come on. What normal kid doesn't want to go to the North Pole?"

"I ain't a kid. And who said I was normal?"

Up ahead of them, the lodge loomed into view. It was a single-floor building with a wide front porch, dark windows, and an annex joined to the main building by a partially covered walkway. The facility was completely fenced in, which kept wildlife out. Behind it, the glassy surface of the ice-covered Churchill River carved a scar through a sea of gleaming white tundra. Other than several outbuildings on the property itself, there were no houses within walking distance, which meant their nearest neighbor was more than five miles away.

"What do you think?" Ethan asked.

"I think it will do perfectly," Emily replied, turning to the others. "Not sure they're going to like it, though."

"Not sure they have much choice."

"You know, if they want to leave, we can't keep them here."

"True, but I'm hoping those with a conscience will support us in any way they can, and those that don't? Well, they'll be first on my list of suspects."

"Which I assume means you're already suspecting the photographer, Tom Oates?"

"Him, maybe. The boyfriend, almost certainly."

"Because?"

"Because statistically, he's the most likely to commit murder."

The words sounded convincing, but he wasn't sure he believed them. He wasn't sure of anything yet, just that one of the most famous women in the world was lying in a body bag at the back of the bus, and somebody in this group might have something to hide. His job was to find out what it was, and he wasn't about to leave Churchill, Manitoba, until he found out exactly what it was.

The driver parked the bus outside the entrance and opened the door. Ethan was the first to set foot outside, and immediately, the sub-zero temperature smacked him in the face like a cold bucket of water.

"Chilly?" Emily asked, laughing as he hastily pulled up the collar of his coat.

"I've experienced colder," he said, trying to catch his breath.

"You mean you've seen it on TV, right?"

"Are you going to help me, or are you going to just stand there and watch?"

Emily rolled the gurney to the ramp at the back of the vehicle as they carefully lowered it onto the ice. With that done, Emily headed toward the makeshift lab while Ethan took control of leading the group inside.

"This place looks like something out of a disaster movie," James said.

"I hope they have some sort of Wi-fi signal," Max replied. "I have at least a dozen clients who are no doubt trying to contact me."

"I'm thinking of using this time to capture some of the stunning landscape," Leo added. "Maybe take some shots of some of us, you know, for prosperity's sake. What do you think, Samantha?"

"I think I'd like to get back to civilization as soon as possible. This place gives me the creeps."

"I don't know," Zoe, the flight attendant, replied. "It seems kind of charming. You know, in a winter wonderland sort of way."

"I just want this whole thing resolved," Lily said. "One way or the other. I think we're all forgetting that Elena Hart was both our employer and our friend. My best friend. She deserves justice."

"And she'll get it," Air Marshal Rodriguez replied, taking her arm. "I promise."

"Don't you think it's a little too late for that, Mike?" Lily replied angrily, wrenching her arm away. "If you'd have done your job on that plane, none of this would have happened."

"What's that supposed to mean?"

"I think you know exactly what it's supposed to mean. You were hired by Max and Sarah to take care of Elena, to make sure she came to no harm during this job, and now she's lying in a body bag, about to be examined by the doctor to find out who or what killed her?"

"So, you're blaming me for that?"

Lily thrust her diminutive frame at the burly marshal. "Yes! I am!"

"Woah," Ethan said, attempting to take control of the volatile situation. "Nobody should be blaming anyone for anything. That's my job, remember, and unless you hadn't realized it, the reason Dr. Carter is examining the body is to find out if anything suspicious occurred. Let's not forget, at the moment, we can't rule out the possibility that Elena Hart died of natural causes."

"At twenty-eight years old?" James asked, "A woman In the prime of her life? Young, healthy people don't just drop dead like that. Not those with the best private health care money can buy."

Ethan had to fight to control his instant reaction to the rich entrepreneur's ridiculously elitist remark. He was really beginning to dislike the guy. "Believe it or not, sir, even the wealthy die."

He turned to the lodge and grimaced. The icy wind cut through him like a serrated knife, sending shivers through his body.

"Might I suggest that, rather than standing out here in our inappropriate clothing and slowly turning into some very large blocks of Arctic ice, we head inside, figure out the lay of the land, and start the interview process properly? With any luck, we might be able to get you all out of here before the winter storms set in."

"I thought you'd never ask," Tom said, pushing past him before slamming through the unlocked door.

Chapter 3

Cold Comfort

The lab was rudimentary at best and barely usable at worst. The wooden structure was really inappropriate for a forensic examination such as this, which is why Emily had called ahead and asked that the local PD erect a crime scene tent in its center and fill it with the necessary tools and implements. At this stage of the investigation, it was absolutely essential that the body be preserved, along with any dust particles, fibers, fingerprints, or debris that might point the finger toward a potential perpetrator.

The room was freezing cold, which is exactly how Emily had asked it to be kept. Without the refrigeration units that were usually used to store a dead body, it was essential that the makeshift lab be kept at below 10 degrees Celsius, thereby drastically slowing the natural process of decomposition. She'd also asked the team to leave her some weatherproof clothing to keep her warm. She had never been so happy to see a fur-lined parka jacket and a pair of thermal gloves in her life. What they said about northern Canada was true. It was about as cold as a hot day in space, and that was lowballing it.

Emily slowly unzipped the body bag and peered down at the lifeless face of somebody she had admired from afar. Elena Hart had been a symbol of female empowerment and liberation, demonstrating to all the young women out there that no matter where you came from or how much money you had, there was no substitute for hard work, a strong moral compass, and fortitude in the face of male chauvinism and an elitist culture. She had been photographed with presidents, prime ministers, Hollywood actors, pop stars, and royalty, and not once had she ever used her power or privilege to publicly put down the little guy. She'd donated hundreds of thousands of dollars to charitable causes, represented UNICEF in some of the world's poorest countries, and spent time with the sick and the elderly. She'd always seemed to be the reluctant celebrity, a woman who'd found herself in a race she couldn't win but one she could manipulate for the good of others and for her own soul. Now, she was just a slab of meat on a gurney. It all seemed such a terrible waste.

"Okay, Elena, my dear," Emily said, her breath coming in fluffy clouds of vapor. "Let's see what we can find."

Firstly, she studied the supermodel's facial features, searching for any kind of infraction or indentation. She checked her throat, her airway, nostrils, and ears, and then moved onto her chest, her shoulders, and then her lower abdomen. Despite initial signs of decomposition, there were no obvious marks or bruising suggesting the victim had been physically assaulted in any way. If anything, the body was in almost perfect condition.

Next, she shone a light into Elena's eyes and looked for burst capillaries, blood spots, or signs of internal bleeding. Satisfied that everything was as it should be, she turned the body over and checked the skull. It wasn't beyond the realm of possibility that Elena had been dealt a severe blow to the back of the head, rendering her unconscious and perhaps causing a bleed in the brain. She cut away some of her luxurious dark hair to get a good look at the skin and skull beneath, but after several minutes of probing and examining, she saw no signs of blunt force trauma.

Cold and a little breathless, she stepped out of the tent and took a moment to consider the possibilities. Maybe Elena Hart hadn't been killed at all. Perhaps this really was a case of a tragic but natural death. It was even possible she'd deliberately ingested something to cause her demise or that an accidental overdose had stopped her heart. Poisoning was also a possibility. The only way she was going to be able to rule those particular scenarios in or out was to perform an internal examination.

She went to the cabinets set up specifically for that eventuality and started removing and setting aside the various implements needed for such an operation: a scalpel, a bone saw, rib shears, a series of sharp blades, gleaming pliers, and sharp scissors. She placed them on the steel trolley beside the gurney and grabbed a gown, gloves, and face mask, approaching the body one final time before proceeding.

Elena was still lying face down, the strands of her hair collected in a dish by her side. Emily wondered what she would make of this if she were still here, looking down on herself as the doctor from the Canadian Special Investigations Unit prepared to inspect her internal organs. What would she say to her? What secrets would she reveal? Did she even know who did this to her or what caused her death? Was she even awake when her heart stopped beating? In these moments, Emily always wished the dead had one last chance to speak before their souls departed. It would make her job so much easier if murder victims could point out their assailants or if the dead could tell the doctors what happened to cause their demise.

It was then that Emily spotted something odd. It was a tiny, innocuous little blemish. She might not have spotted it at all if it wasn't for the section of hair she'd shaved away at the base of Elena's neck. A small dot of blood, no larger than a pinprick, at a point halfway between the base of the victim's skull and the lower part of her neck. She leaned in and took a closer look, pulling across an illuminated magnification lens on a telescopic arm so she could really see what she was looking at.

"Well, I'll be damned," she said as she made a note of the size and exact location of the puncture wound. There really had been a killer on that airplane, and what's more, they were smart. This wasn't a crime of passion or a clumsy assault. This had been a premeditated, well-thought-out execution—the cause of which they had tried with some success to conceal.

The only question now was, what kind of powerful drug had been injected into Elena Hart's bloodstream to cause her to literally die in her seat?

***

The wind outside whistled across the barren tundra as a cluster of snow flakes flittered past the window. The sky was gradually darkening and so was the mood in the cabin.

Ethan watched as the group took their places in the living quarters, buddying up in the way groups of people usually do in stressful, constrained situations. The agent, Max, was deep in dialogue with the project manager, Sarah, while the freelance photographer, Leo, huddled beside the no-

nonsense stylist, Sam. Lily, the makeup artist, comforted Elena's partner, James, while Air Marshal Rodriguez held an intense conversation with the Gulfstream's captain, Jeremy Watts. The flight attendant, Zoe, looked out of sorts and flustered, and so their social media leak, co-pilot Jason Meyer, tried to redeem himself by comforting her. The only passenger who set himself apart from the others was Elena's personal documentarian and cameraman, Tom Oates. He looked completely unsettled and deeply annoyed about being so severely inconvenienced.

Ethan took it all in, making mental notes as he sat silently, swirling the remains of his espresso in a paper cup. The first thing he'd been taught by his mentor and long-time friend, Charles Schaeffer, the head of Toronto's highly specialized detective training academy, was that people rarely told you the complete truth with words, and so you had to let them show you what they were really feeling through their actions. Tom was giving him all sorts of unsettling vibes, and that was important. It meant he was either involved in some way or he knew something. The way the Air Marshal was acting was also interesting, as were the agent's whisperings into the ear of the project manager. It all gave Ethan the impression that some of these people had been playing at being Elena Hart's friends when what they were really doing was looking out for themselves. Very few of them looked upset. In fact, the overriding sensation Ethan got was one of self-protection. This was a group who had lost their link to a lifestyle they loved, and they didn't know what to do about that.

"Okay," he said, standing abruptly and heading to one of the small meeting rooms at the far end of the living quarters. "Firstly I'd like to interview the flight crew to eliminate them from my inquiries. After that, I'll interview each of you in turn. Sit tight everybody, this is going to take some time."

***

After his discussions with the captain, co-pilot, and flight attendant had been completed, Ethan made the decision to let the three of them leave. They had all been vetted by the airline, had flown that airplane multiple times, and had no known association with Elena Hart. On top of that, none of them had a motive. If the supermodel had been murdered, Ethan was sure that the perpetrator came from within one of her entourage, not the people tasked with flying her to Manitoba.

Their departure did not go down well with the others.

"Hey, how come they get to leave?" Max cried. "What makes them so special?"

"Nothing but circumstance, Mr. Roth," Ethan replied. "But don't worry, we know where to find them if we need them. Now, Mr. Bateman, if you wouldn't mind following me."

"Of course," James said, eyeing Lily as he grabbed his glasses. "Whatever you say. Do I need to bring anything?"

"Just your thoughts."

Ethan opened the door and stood aside as James walked in. Behind him, the others looked on in horror. Ethan guessed that for them, this had all just gotten real.

"Take a seat," he said, setting a recording device on the small table and placing himself directly opposite the interviewee. "Just so you're aware, I'll be recording all of these interviews so that I have a clear record of our conversations. Of course, none of the recordings will be admissible into evidence if we do find something incriminating as you're not under arrest."

"And neither should I be," James said, startled. "I've done nothing wrong."

Ethan nodded, ignoring his protestations as he hit record on the machine. "Can you start by telling me your name, age, and occupation?"

"Sure, although I'm sure you know all of this." The entrepreneur shuffled uncomfortably in his chair and cleared his throat. "My name is James Bateman. I'm thirty-two years old, which is not relevant to this investigation, and I'm the successful owner of several high-end nightclubs in Chicago and Detroit."

"Successful, as in they make a lot of money?"

"What? Yes, that, and we also have some highly respected clientele."

"Such as?"

"We keep our client list confidential, I'm afraid."

"You know I could subpoena it, right?"

James's eye twitched. "Why would you do that?"

"If I feel it's important, I'll do whatever it takes to find the truth."

James ran his hands through his expertly coiffured hair, which was a telltale sign of discomfort. "Look, if you must know, the club on the east side of Chicago is attended by the mayor's chief counsel, Arty Lofthouse."

"You mean the strip club, I presume."

"We prefer to call them gentleman's clubs."

"I'm sure you do."

Ethan let the silence hang in the air, watching as the self-proclaimed nightclub king of the Midwest chewed on his tongue. There was no doubt he was hiding something. Ethan just had to find out what.

"You know I'm the grieving partner here?" James said eventually. "I mean, you do know that, right? Elena and I, we were in love. She was my north star, my one. I just can't believe..." he slammed his hand on the table, his face screwed into a tight ball. "I just can't believe she's gone."

"Yes, about that," Ethan said. "How strong would you say your relationship was in the months leading up to Ms. Hart's death? Was it healthy? Have you had any difficulties?"

"Completely strong. Bullet-proof strong. We were inseparable."

"And yet, not six weeks ago, you went on a four-day trip to the Southwest without Ms. Hart."

If the nightclub owner was shocked by the level of Ethan's homework, he didn't show it. "It was a business trip."

"But you just told me all your clubs are in the Midwest."

"We were looking to expand."

Ethan made another note, this time writing deliberately and slowly and allowing his subject to think things over.

"Can you tell me your recollection of the events during flight XZ3791's journey from Chicago O'Hare to Churchill, Manitoba, specifically any conversations you had with Ms. Hart, anything she may have said that could be pertinent, and also any significant incidents you can recall that may be important to our investigation—and please, don't leave anything out, even if you think it's unimportant. At present, everything and anything could prove to be essential."

James thought for a moment. "It really was a pretty mundane few hours. Elena was the first to board because, of course, she was the star of the show, and then I followed shortly after."

"Were you seated beside Ms. Hart."

"I was."

"In row three?"

"I think that's right. Yes."

"And which of the passengers were seated closest to you."

James ran a hand across his chin. "Well, let's see. The scruffy photographer with the attitude, Tom, was seated across the aisle to my right, and ahead of him, again in the next aisle, was Air Marshal Rodriguez."

"And behind you?"

"Sarah was behind us, and Elena's agent, Max, was in the row across from her."

"So let me get this straight. Directly behind you was Sarah Locke, Ms. Hart's PR spokesperson and the project manager for this trip."

James's eyes narrowed at the question. "Yes. Do you think that's important?"

"As I said, anything and everything could be essential."

James nodded, clearly starting to form opinions in his own mind. That was always the danger with direct questions such as these. They often gave the interviewee more to think about, and perhaps more ways to deflect the interview.

"At the back of the plane, in the next cabin, were the freelance photographer, Leo, and Elena's stylist, Samantha. If you ask me, those two have something going on."

"I didn't," Ethan replied, but he noted the observation anyway. "So that just leaves the flight crew and one other person you haven't mentioned. Can you tell me where Lily Craven was in all of this?"

James shook his head. "Sorry, yes. I should have included Lily. She was originally going to be seated in the next cabin, but she came up and sat with us."

"By us, you mean..."

"Elena and I. She and Elena are...*were* very close."

"They were best friends?"

"Of sorts. They've known each other a long time. Lily has been Elena's makeup artist since she started to make a name for herself seven or eight years ago."

"So, this must have hit her pretty hard?"

"It's hit the both of us hard," James replied. "I don't think I'll ever get over the loss of Elena."

The way he said the last part of the sentence, almost too matter-of-fact, struck Ethan as off as if he was reciting a statistic or a line from a play.

"And when did you notice something was wrong with Ms. Hart?"

James seemed distracted for a moment, staring at the wall as if he'd seen something interesting.

"Mr. Bateman, if this is too much for you, we can take a break."

"No, no, it's fine. What was the question again?"

"I asked when you noticed something was wrong with your partner."

He shook his head, apparently angered by the line of inquiry. "I didn't. I wasn't even anywhere near her."

"What do you mean by that?"

"Exactly what I just said. Elena hates flying, so Lily slipped her a couple of Valiums to help her relax. She fell asleep shortly after takeoff, so a few of us headed to the rear cabin so she could rest."

"So, Ms. Hart was on her own when she passed?"

"No. The Air Marshal was still in his seat, as far as I know, and Tom never joins in with the group. The guy's a serial loner with a chip on his shoulder as big as Mount Rainier."

"Interesting."

"Yeah, maybe you should be talking to those guys instead of quizzing me."

"It's my job to quiz people, Mr. Bateman."

"Yeah, but you seem to be throwing accusations around about my business and my relationship with the woman I loved. If you really wanna know who I think killed Elena, it's that lowlife agent of hers, Roth. It's no secret Elena's been looking around for someone else to represent her ever since the guy was caught in the back of an RV with two hookers and a large bag of coke. Ever since that, their relationship has never been the same."

Ethan made another note, but not before he spotted something.

"That ring on your finger, the one you keep twisting around as if you're afraid you might lose it. Did Ms. Hart buy you that?"

"She did. Why?"

"No reason. Just interested." Except he did have a reason. It was what Charlie Schaeffer used to call the *band of guilt*. In almost every instance, if an interviewee is continually distracted by an item of jewelry, then they're hiding something, and it was usually big. James Bateman had told Ethan an awful lot during the interview, but as predicted, his words weren't the most telling piece of this engagement. There was much more to Elena

Hart's long-time boyfriend than designer clothes and expensive jewelry, and none of it was good. Ethan just had to bide his time, and eventually, the truth would come spilling out.

***

Ethan spoke to Lily, Max, and Tom before the day was out, probing at some of the things James Bateman had told him but also letting them tell him what they wanted to share. These early engagements were always an exercise in laying the foundations, building relationships, and firing a few shots across the bow.

Lily had been emotional during the whole process, constantly reminding Ethan that she and Elena Hart were the best of friends and that if she had known what was about to happen, she would never have allowed Elena to accept the Churchill assignment. When he asked her about what she thought had happened, she was less forthcoming than James, preferring instead to stand as a character witness for every single occupant of the Gulfstream G620. In her view, not one of them had it in them to commit such a heinous act. Ethan had to remind her, as he'd had to remind James, that so far, nobody had said a murder had been committed.

Max was the bullish character Ethan had read all about, entering the room like a tornado, throwing himself into his chair, and commanding the room. He was filled with opinions about each and every one of the passengers, suggesting that James was only with Elena for the fame and money, that Lily was a hanger-on, and that Tom was a cantankerous has-been who'd been clutching onto Elena's coattails ever since he'd lost a high profile job documenting a blockbuster Hollywood movie due to the partner in his business being arrested for extortion. When it came to Elena, he was more guarded, complimenting her on the way she'd risen from obscurity in such a short space of time but criticizing her inability to see people for who they really were and suggesting her high moral standards had lost them both some very lucrative offers. However, it was his parting comment that left Ethan feeling cold.

"You know," Max said, turning to Ethan, his cheeks flushed. "It's going to be hard to replace someone like Elena Hart. She's been my number-one client for almost a decade. She was my 'A' game, the ace in my pack. People came to me to represent them because of my relationship with the world's premier supermodel, and now she's gone. I have no idea what I'm going to do."

Ethan took that as the one moment of sincerity in their otherwise banal exchange, but it was also the one that disgusted him the most. To Max Roth, Elena Hart was just an asset, a number on his balance sheet. He wasn't upset that a young woman had tragically lost her life. He was upset that his business had just taken an extraordinary hit to its bottom line.

When Tom came in for his interview, he brought a sense of doom and impending catastrophe with him. They say that a person's mood can affect the whole room, and Tom Oates practically embodied that phrase. He was the kind of man who looked like he needed a haircut, a shave, a good wash, and a change of clothes. If James Bateman was the epitome of grooming and sophistication, Tom Oates was the direct opposite, and it wasn't just his appearance that set the tone of their meeting. It was his attitude. Max had been right. Tom was cynical about everything, pissed off about the situation, and angry that Ethan had the audacity to think that he could possibly have had anything to do with Elena's death.

"As I told you already," Tom said, practically spitting his words. "I was reading. I barely paid any attention to what was going on around me, least of all to Elena's dealings with her army of attention seekers."

"So, you're not a fan?"

"Of the type of vapid, shallow lifestyle Elena had? Or of the people she chose to associate herself with?"

"Either?"

"No, and no. I like neither."

"But you remained in her employment for a considerable amount of time."

"I'm a photographer and documentarian, Detective. Jobs for artists like myself do not grow on trees. We take what we can get, and for me, the longevity of the assignment with Elena Hart was fortuitous—it paid the bills—but it wasn't necessarily artistically rewarding."

His candor shocked Ethan. If he was speaking truthfully, he clearly had plenty of motivation for killing the supermodel, not least his frustration that his artistic talents were being wasted on what he called 'shallow mediocrity. It all gave Ethan a lot of food for thought, and he planned to mull it over while he broke the news to the group that they would all be holed up there for the night.

As predicted, it didn't go down well.

"You have to be kidding?" Sarah Locke said. "We all have lives to get back to, you know?"

"I do," Ethan replied. "But it's getting late. We're all tired, and I still need to talk to most of you."

"But what about those of us you've already interviewed?" James asked, looking increasingly agitated. "Why can't we leave?"

"Because this is an iterative process, and as I gather information, it's almost certain that I'll have to speak to you all again."

"And what about Elena?" Lily asked, her hands shaking. "What happens to her body?"

"Well, she's in the lab next door. Dr. Carter is carrying out some investigations as we speak, which will hopefully tell us a little more about what really happened to Ms. Hart."

Fortunately, the lodge had enough bunks for up to twenty people, so everybody was allocated a bed to sleep in. The bedrooms housed four people each, so Ethan watched with interest as the group negotiated who would bunk down with whom. Unsurprisingly, Samantha and Leo headed for the same room, as did Lily and James. After Max and Sarah decided to share with the Air Marshal, it meant only Tom was left out in the cold.

Ethan faced the window and watched as the clouds rolled in and the dark lips of night kissed the icy landscape. Subconsciously, he pulled his jacket around his body, trying to keep away the chill now seeping into his bones.

***

The kitchen was a mass of activity as everybody took turns creating something edible out of canned foods, noodles, dried rice, and assorted frozen foods. Nobody went hungry.

Ethan, on the other hand, grabbed the sandwich he'd bought at the airport and headed into one of the side offices. To his surprise, Emily joined him.

"You're done?" he asked, biting down on a pastrami on rye.

"My initial examination is complete," she replied. "Much more to do tomorrow."

"And what did you find?"

Emily extracted an apple and a protein bar from her own bag. "Nothing conclusive yet, but I did find something very interesting."

She took a bite from her apple and sat there chewing, looking out at the rapidly darkening sky.

"Are you going to fill me in, or do you plan to keep me guessing?" he asked.

"You don't like the suspense?"

"Not really, no."

Emily took another bite and smirked.

"You remember that case we took in Montreal? The one where the killer worked with animals?"

"The farm slayings? Yeah, of course I remember it. The guy was a complete nut-job."

"Right. Vic Grossman, the farmer who liked to hang his victims on meat hooks. Anyway, do you remember how he killed the first woman?"

Ethan sat back in his chair and scratched his head. "Didn't he anesthetize her somehow?"

"He did. Lidocaine hydrochloride, the same anesthetic he used on his cattle. Now, I'm not saying that's what happened here, but I can say that something was injected into the base of Ms. Hart's skull."

"Because?"

"Because I found this." She tossed a photograph onto the table, which showed the puncture mark she'd located after shaving Elena Hart's hair.

Ethan puffed out his cheeks. "She was murdered?"

"I can't say for certain, but the evidence is certainly pointing in that direction." She held up the photograph. "It's almost a sure thing that something was injected into Elena's bloodstream during the flight, and given the location of this mark, it's very unlikely she did this to herself."

Ethan let the facts swill around inside his brain. This confirmed that somebody in the cabin was responsible for the supermodel's death, which meant this now had to be treated as a murder investigation. It put a new level of formality on proceedings.

"Will you tell them?" Emily asked.

"About the puncture wound?"

She nodded in reply.

He thought about the question. What would telling the group get him, other than unnecessarily causing unease among those that were innocent?

"Not for now. Let's see if anyone volunteers information that might suggest they know something we haven't mentioned."

"Like Montreal?"

"Exactly like Montreal."

Ethan's cell phone rang. It was the Detective Superintendent, Rami Cortez.

"Chief," he said.

"Ethan. We may have a problem."

Ethan eyed Emily, who had moved onto her protein bar. She nibbled on the corner, turning up her nose as if it were the most disgusting thing she'd ever tasted.

"Go on."

"The leak from the co-pilot. His post seems to have gone...how do these kids say it these days?"

"Viral?"

"That's it. Viral, like a pandemic. Over half a million hits at the last count. Intel suggests there are armies of reporters on their way to Churchill."

"Good luck getting here. It looks like a storm front's moving in."

"You know these guys. It'll take a lot more than a few snowflakes and an icy railroad track to stop them."

Ethan shook his head. The chief had a way of underestimating things, particularly extreme weather conditions.

"I think we'll be okay."

There was a heavy sigh down the line. "This thing has the potential to blow up into something way out of our control, Ethan. We need to shut it down fast before the media get their claws into it. You understand what I'm saying?"

"I hear you, Chief. I hear you loud and clear."

"We need a cause of death, and assuming this is what we think it is, we need to find the murderer. When superstars like Elena Hart die unexpectedly, the whole world wants to know what happened, and they want to know it, like yesterday. There's no time to waste here. I have the governor breathing down my neck, and I'm pretty sure the Prime Minister himself will be taking a keen interest in the case. Let's give them what they want, Ethan. Let's give them a headline."

The call ended just as Ethan was about to remind his boss that he wasn't a complete novice, and that he and Emily were working just as fast as they could in less than ideal conditions.

"The media floodgates are opening, aren't they," Emily said.

"The political ones, too. You know, I'd be pissed at that co-pilot if I didn't think something like this was bound to happen anyway. It seems that all people care about these days is how many followers they have."

"Hey, not me. My Facebook page only has one subscriber—my mom—and I'm not even sure she knows how to access it."

Ethan laughed. Emily had that effect on him. He could always count on her to improve his mood, even if he was in the bleakest of places. He thought of Rebecca, of the months after her death, of the deep, dark hole he'd found himself in, of the anger that had churned up his insides like an electric drill. When he'd eventually emerged from that black place, he'd pushed himself into a career where he knew he could do better than the guys that were tasked with finding his fiancée's killer, and someway down the line, he met Emily, a woman who brought a smile to every room, and a sense of calm to the angriest of waters.

"You know this is going be tough," he said. "These guys aren't friends, not really, and they all have their own little secrets. If we're going to unlock the vaults inside their heads, we're going to need a key, starting with the chemical that was injected into the base of Elena Hart's skull."

Emily leaned back in her chair and folded her hands behind her head. "Don't worry. I'll find it."

Ethan glared out the window as the snow started to fall a little harder. He hoped his partner was right. Otherwise, they were in for a long week—a week that might start to feel like forever.

Chapter 4

The Lodge of Secrets

That night, Emily dreamed of Elena Hart's lifeless body rising from the autopsy table, crossing the short walkway between the two buildings, and entering her bedroom, a needle gripped in her slowly decomposing hands. Just as the sharp tip pressed against Emily's throat, she sat up, suddenly aware of somebody moving around in the living quarters.

She let her eyes adjust to the darkness and looked across at Ethan's bunk. His chest rose and fell with the relaxed rhythm of deep sleep. She had no idea how he did it. No matter how tough the case or how disturbing the grisly details, he could sleep anywhere. She, on the other hand, was constantly restless, running things back and forth in her mind, trying to put all the pieces of the puzzle together. It was like her brain was constantly in overdrive.

There was another noise, this time a little louder. She rose from her bed and let what little light was coming through the window guide her to the door. She opened it a crack and looked into the large living space. A dark shadow stood by the front door.

"Hello?" she whispered. "Who's there?"

The shadow turned slowly, revealing an impish face and sharp eyes. Emily was surprised and a little relieved to see Lily Craven standing there in a long nightgown.

"Can't sleep either, eh?"

Lily shook her head. "I'm not a good sleeper. My doctor prescribes me maximum strength liquid Valium just so I can get a few hours of shut-eye each night. A dose of that, coupled with a shot of vodka, and I'm out cold."

"So why can't you sleep? No Valium?"

Lily smiled. "No vodka." She turned to the window. "I keep thinking about Elena, too, out there all on her own. She must be so cold and so afraid."

Emily let her words hang. In her experience, correcting someone's grip on reality when they were mourning someone they cared for deeply was almost always a mistake.

"You want a coffee?"

Lily nodded. "I might as well. I don't think I could sleep, even if I tried."

Emily went to the dispensing machine and filled two cups. "The good thing about working for the police department is that the coffee was free. I can't say it's the best caffeine you'll have this year or even this week, but it's warm, and it's strong."

Lily took the cup and hugged it within her tiny fingers as if it were the only source of heat in the whole of Churchill. "Warm and strong is good."

They took a seat on the sofa, and Emily nodded toward the lab outside. "You two were good friends, I assume?"

"The best."

"How did you meet?"

Lily's eyes glazed over. "Elena and I were working at the same local fashion exhibition in downtown Detroit. We used to model in the same circles and compete in the same competitions. I did pretty well for myself when I was younger, but Elena, you know? She was something else. I got to know her better during some modeling shoots we both attended upstate, and I always thought she looked like she was going places. She was so beautiful, so graceful. I thought she was way out of my league."

"But you took the gig as her makeup artist?"

"Elena could be pretty convincing when she wanted to be. This was before Elena had a project manager and a personal stylist, so her team was basically Max and a young kid who ran around getting her coffee and snacks. Anyway, when her makeup artist let her down, I convinced her I could be the one to get her out of trouble, and the rest, as they say, is history."

"That's pretty bold."

"Maybe. It was either bold or stupid. Either way, it worked, and I got the job. Elena and me, we hit it off straight away. I was shocked to learn we grew up less than six blocks apart in Brightmoor. We came from less than nothing, and yet here we were, working one of the most up-and-coming fashion gigs in town. We bonded over that, and so she hired me as her permanent makeup artist right there on the spot."

"And you've never looked back?"

She smiled. "Sure, we had our tough times, and when we got down to an argument, there was no holding us back. But we were sisters, and like all sisters, we fought."

"What did you fight about?"

Lily paused and sipped her coffee. For a moment, Emily thought her question had been too direct and that their friendly, early morning conversation was about to take an unexpected turn.

"Work mainly," Lily said. "The jobs she was taking. As I said, Max is a pretty convincing guy, persistent too, and he worked Elena real hard, which meant I had to work real hard, too. Sometimes too hard. When you're with somebody every day, week in, week out, traveling all over the country and sometimes overseas, you can get a little sick of each other. That happened now and again with Elena and me, but as I said, we were sisters, and we always made up after a fight. It was the reason we stayed together for so long."

"And I assume with these big jobs came big money?"

"I wouldn't know that," Lily countered a little too eagerly. "Elena was the star of the show, I was just a supporting artist. I got paid the same for every job, no matter how big or how important it was."

"That must have frustrated you."

Lily shrugged. "It comes with the territory. The talent gets the main meal. The rest of us get the scraps."

Emily couldn't help but notice the curl in Lily's upper lip or the flicker in her eyes. She was clearly not as happy with the arrangement as she was making out.

"Tell me about James," Emily asked, trying to slip in the question she really wanted to ask without being too obvious. "Did the two of you get on?"

"Elena liked him, and that was all that mattered to me."

"But his presence must have affected your relationship with Elena. Are you telling me there was never any friction between you, even though he took up so much of your best friend's time?"

Lily shook her head. "Not really. Sure, Elena became a little more distracted with him around, but I was used to that. There were always people buzzing around her. The more famous she got, the larger the entourage, and the larger the entourage, the more the general public wanted access to her."

"So, she and James, they never fought?"

Lily seemed to flinch at the question. "If you're asking if James killed her, I'd have to say I have no idea. Maybe you should ask him."

"I'm not accusing anyone here."

"Sure seems like you are."

The sudden shift in Lily's demeanor was startling, so Emily tried to dampen the flames. "If I offended you, I'm sorry. It wasn't my intention."

"And yet you did it anyway."

"I'm not the enemy here, Lily. I just want to get to the truth."

The makeup artist stood sharply, slamming her cup onto the table before storming back to her room. "Then I suggest you do a better job and start digging in the right places."

"Then give me a clue! Where should I begin?"

Lily turned back toward her, her body trembling with emotion. "Maybe the guy who manipulated his way onto that plane, the one person who none of us had even met until yesterday. Maybe you should start with him."

***

Ethan listened to Emily's tale of her early morning exchange with Elena Hart's best friend and confidante, followed by the bizarrely emotional end to their encounter. Lily Craven's defense of Elena's boyfriend was interesting, but the standout moment for Ethan was her parting comment. Aside from the crew, there was only one other person on that flight who the passengers weren't familiar with, and that was the guy who was hired to make sure Elena Hart made it safely to Churchill and back.

After some background research, which Ethan conducted over the internet and through a few hastily arranged telephone calls, he dusted himself down and took a deep breath.

"Morning, everybody," he said to the group. They were all now fully awake, eagerly devouring the pancakes that Samantha and Leo had volunteered to cook for them and keen to get the remaining interviews over with. "I hope you all slept well."

"Not me," Tom said. "That mattress is about as uncomfortable as a bathtub full of crushed glass."

"Speak for yourself. I slept like a baby," Max replied. "But they say the innocent rest easily."

"What the hell are you implying?" Tom snipped back.

"Okay, okay," Ethan said as Max offered a smug grin. "So first up, I'd like to start with Air Marshal Rodriguez. If you can follow me, sir. The rest of you, enjoy your food and I promise, I'll get to you just as soon as I can."

The ex-soldier looked stunned about being next on the roster but dutifully set down his knife and fork and did as he was asked.

"I assume this is just a formality," he said, closing the office door and taking a seat. The chair beneath him looked tiny against his large frame. "You can't seriously think I had anything to do with this, not with us both working in the same field."

"Which is?" Ethan asked, switching on the recording device.

"The job of getting criminals off our streets and keeping people safe."

"How long have you been an Air Marshal?" Ethan asked, choosing to ignore Rodriguez's misguided attempt at forming some sort of professional bond with him.

"A little over two years."

"So, not long."

"Long enough. Heck, in this job, every day can seem like a lifetime, am I right?"

"You and I have very different jobs, Air Marsha. I don't think we can really compare notes."

Rodriguez seemed disarmed by Ethan's counter. "I'm a professional who was just trying to carry out his job to the best of his ability."

"And yet Ms. Hart is now in a mortuary being examined by a professional medical examiner."

"That isn't my fault."

"I never said it was, but if someone is given a job to do, and that job isn't carried out to the client's satisfaction, then it has to be deemed a failure. In this case, you were employed to keep Elena Hart safe, and now she's dead."

Rodriguez clenched his teeth, offended by the accusation, which was exactly what Ethan had intended. His comments were designed to put his interviewee on the back foot. If Rodriguez really was implicated in some way, the best method to get him to reveal more than he wanted to was to heighten his fractious state of emotional distress.

"How long have you known Elena Hart?"

"Less than two days."

"And who employed you for this job."

"The project manager for the assignment."

"And in this case, that was Sarah Locke, right?"

"That's right."

"And what's your relationship with Ms. Locke?"

Rodriguez shook his head, confused. "Meaning?"

"Meaning, how long have you known her, and in what capacity?"

Rodriguez glared at his hands, which were clasped together in front of him. "We met in a bar a few weeks ago."

"So, you were dating?"

"Not exactly."

Ethan set down his pen. "So, fill me in. The two of you met in a bar, and you hooked up. Is that what you're telling me?"

"Something like that."

"And because of this...episode, Ms. Locke considered you the perfect guy to take care of her world-famous, extremely sought-after client."

"As I said, I've been an Air Marshal for a couple of years. Joined after I left active service, and because of that Ms. Locke....*Sarah*...thought that I'd be a good fit."

Ethan made a point of checking his notes, letting Rodriguez stew for a couple of minutes more than was absolutely necessary.

"Says here that your social media account includes some photographs and comments related to Ms. Hart that were posted back when you were overseas. Is that right?"

Rodriguez's head jerked as if Ethan had slapped him across the face. "How did you get access to that information?"

"That's the thing about social media posts," Ethan said, grinning. "They're considered public domain."

The Air Marshal's face turned a deep shade of scarlet.

"I also called your ex-commanding officer in the 38th Infantry Division and had a long conversation with him. He's a nice guy. In fact, he told me something very interesting about the room you shared with Corporal...Heskie, is that right?"

"Lenny Heskie, yeah. We were good buddies."

"Right. Well, First Lieutenant Murray was very helpful, filling me in on how you pinned some very specific pictures up on the wall beside your bed, something you were reprimanded for on several occasions."

"I know where you're going with this, and you're wrong."

"I'm not going anywhere with it, Air Marshal. I'm just trying to establish the facts as they relate to this case."

"And how is this particular fact relevant?"

Ethan leaned forward, holding eye contact with his subject. "Isn't it true that those pictures—the ones that you risked your military career over by constantly defacing the walls of your dorm—were magazine images of a barely clothed Ms. Elena Hart?"

Rodriguez glared at the detective. "Just because I liked the way she looked doesn't mean I killed her."

Ethan raised his hands. "I never insinuated that, neither did I accuse you."

"But that's the direction of this interview, isn't it? Do I need a lawyer here?"

"Only if you've done something wrong, and so far, all I've highlighted is that you were a fan of the deceased."

The Air Marshal folded his arms. "She was one of the most famous supermodels on the planet, Detective. Show me a man who doesn't know who Elena Hart was, and then show me another man who wasn't taken in by her elegance and beauty."

Ethan conceded the point before changing tack. "This Corporal Lenny Heskie. Tell me about him."

"What do you want to know? Lenny's a good guy."

"And you two were close?"

"Still are."

"So close that he asked to change rooms during your last tour."

Again, Rodriguez jerked in his seat. "We had a minor disagreement."

"That isn't how Lieutenant Murray tells it. He says that Corporal Heskie was uncomfortable with continuing to be your bunk buddy, and that he was creeped out by you. In fact, he claimed—the lieutenant's words, not mine—that you had started to become so attached to him that you were bordering on being obsessive."

"I don't recall it like that."

"I see. And how do you recall it?"

"That Lenny could be a little cold, a little hard to like, and for that reason, we agreed to change sleeping arrangements."

The Air Marshal's demeanor had shifted. His straight face had returned, and his conversational tone had become flat and emotionless.

"Would you say you don't make friends easily, Air Marshal Rodriguez?"

"I'd say the army can have an effect on a person's ability to relate to members of the public. Trauma can have that effect on the human mind, particularly when it's sustained, day in and day out. Remind me, where did you say you served?"

"I didn't."

"Ah, that's right. You never felt the need to fight for your country."

"It wasn't my calling."

"For people like you, it never is. You know, I read about your fiancée."

Now, it was Ethan's turn to flinch.

"She was killed, wasn't she? Murdered? Did they ever catch the guy who did it?"

Ethan didn't respond. He just glared at the Air Marshal, fighting his natural impulse to grab the guy around the throat and shake him.

"Oh, that's right, they didn't. The local police force bungled the investigation, and your guy made it away, right?"

Again, Ethan didn't respond.

"But I bet you know who did it. I bet you have a good idea, and I bet it takes every ounce of strength you have to stop yourself from jumping on a plane, heading straight to that guy's front door, and beating the living crap out of him until he draws his last breath. Am I right?"

"I think we should get back to Elena Hart's untimely death."

The Air Marshal grinned. "Yeah, I thought so. You just can't bear it, can you? You see, that's the kind of trauma I'm talking about, Detective Steele. The kind of pain that never leaves you, never quite lets you take a breath without punching you in the stomach and knocking the wind out of your sails. You accuse me of being unable to form lasting relationships, and I fire that accusation back at you. We're the same, you and I, even if you're too proud to admit it."

***

Ethan took some time between interviews to regather his thoughts. There was no doubt that the Air Marshal had a longstanding obsession with Elena Hart, but despite it ringing an alarm bell, he knew it didn't make him her killer. He was also smarter than he looked, thoroughly researching Ethan's background and using it to get under his skin, destabilizing the interview process. It had worked, and shortly after the exchange, Ethan had ended his questioning, choosing to make a tactical retreat rather than lose his cool.

He looked across the walkway to the lab, hoping that the door would open and Emily would appear, a piece of paper in hand revealing the cause of the supermodel's death. It would make his job so much easier. It would give him something to slip into his questioning, something to throw the interviewees off guard. For now, they were remaining tight-lipped, giving him just enough to answer his queries but not enough to allow him to draw any worthwhile conclusions.

Just as he was about to call in the next interviewee, he received a message from the office. He'd asked the more junior members of the investigating team in Toronto to scour through the security camera footage from the airport just prior to take-off, and one of them had found something interesting—very interesting, in fact. It was so interesting that he switched interviewees at the last minute.

"Lily?" he said, entering the living quarters where a few of the group were watching TV and drinking coffee. "If it's okay, I'd like to go over a few things from yesterday."

"Already?" she asked, looking a little sheepish. "I thought you were going to interview everybody else first."

"Unfortunately, in an investigation such as this, things can change in an instant," he replied. "It won't take long, I promise."

Lily reluctantly followed him, shooting a nervous glance over her shoulder as Ethan ushered her through the doorway. Behind her, James Bateman's dark eyes peered over the rim of his steaming cup, watching their every move.

"Care to fill me in?" Lily asked. "Because I can tell you, as I'm the only passenger to have been questioned twice, everybody out there will be forming their own misguided opinions."

"I'm aware of that," Ethan replied, "But that's the way these things are, I'm afraid. In almost all the murders I've investigated, the people involved turn on each other eventually."

Lily sat back sharply. "Murder? Has that been confirmed?"

Ethan studied her reaction. Was she as surprised as he would have suspected her to be, or did she know more than she was letting on?

"It's looking that way."

"Well, either she was killed, or she wasn't. It can't be that difficult to find out. Isn't that why you brought the doctor here? To examine Elena's body? To find out what happened to her?"

"Ms. Craven, I can assure you, when we have something concrete to share with you, we will."

"Then why the hell have you dragged me back in here?" She looked back at the door, swept her hair aside, and fiddled anxiously with her hands.

"Ms. Craven, if you would like some time to calm down, I'm happy to step out of the room."

Lily chewed at a fingernail before taking a deep breath and shaking her head. "No, I'm fine. Say what you gotta say."

"I wanted to ask you some more about your relationship with Ms. Hart's boyfriend, James Bateman."

"I thought we went over that yesterday."

"Yes, we did. I took some notes from my audio recording. Would you mind if I refer to those?"

Lily shrugged. "Go ahead if you need to."

"Thanks. It's just that I like to be thorough and recall precisely what was said. I think perhaps I'm borderline OCD."

He pulled his notebook from his pocket, made a point of thumbing through the pages, and then set it open at the section marked *Lily*. While he was doing this, the makeup artist watched him intently, occasionally looking toward the exit.

"So, this is it," he said eventually. "You told me that you and Mr. Bateman barely spoke, but when you did, you had a courteous relationship but no more."

"That's the truth."

"And you also said you thought Ms. Hart was too good for Mr. Bateman, but you never interfered because, and I quote, '*who am I to judge. I've always had the relationships from hell, and that's an understatement.*'"

"Also, the truth. Sadly."

Ethan reached for his tablet and scrolled through the files sent to him from Toronto. He located an mp4 file labeled '*Gate 13.*'

"Can I ask what you make of this, Ms. Craven?"

Ethan held the tablet up so that Lily could see it before hitting 'play.' Within a couple of seconds, the video file began. It depicted a doorway that led out onto the airfield. In the distance, Ethan could see the G650 on the asphalt and a number of people boarding the plane. Elena Hart was one of those people. After a few moments, James Bateman stepped into the shot. He was still inside the airport terminal and appeared to be beckoning to someone just off-screen. Ethan looked up at Lily and watched the growing unease start to take hold of her. The color had drained from her complexion.

James beckoned once more, and after a few moments of inactivity, a young woman appeared. She had her back to the camera as she slipped her arms around James's waist and leaned into him. The couple's lips met as they kissed. They stood that way with their arms around each other, kissing tenderly, before the woman pointed to the plane and then urged James to board. As he grabbed his bag and walked across the asphalt, she turned to the camera. There was no doubting the sharp nose or high cheekbones.

"How long have you and Mr. Bateman been having an affair, Ms. Craven?"

"It's not like that. It's...it's..." her voice cracked as her lips trembled. Tears glistened in her eyes.

"Then please, educate me because from where I'm sitting, your description of your relationship with Mr. Bateman seems entirely fictional. In fact, the two of you seem very familiar with each other's bodies."

"You're making it sound sordid, which it isn't."

"But that is you kissing Elena Hart's partner, Mr. James Bateman, right?"

Lily nodded.

"The same person you told me you had a merely courteous relationship with?"

She nodded again.

"Does that look merely courteous to you, Ms. Craven?"

"I know how it looks, and I know how it makes me seem, but you have to understand, Elena and James, they weren't happy. Their relationship was killing both of them."

"And yet, that's not how you described it yesterday."

"Because I didn't want that information to get out into the public domain. It wouldn't be fair to Elena. It wouldn't be fair to either of them."

Ethan pointed to the screen. "And is this?"

Her tears came at that point. Her shoulders heaved as she buried her face in her hands and sobbed, her muffled cries filling the tiny interview room. After grabbing a box of tissues and allowing the sobs to subside, Ethan decided to pause.

He had somebody else to speak with.

***

"It was nothing. Just a fling," James said, handing the tablet back to Ethan almost nonchalantly.

"But Ms. Hart wasn't aware of it?"

"No way. Would you tell your wife that kind of thing?"

Ethan chose not to answer the question.

"No, what I did in my own time was my business and the same was true for Elena."

"So, Ms. Hart was having an affair, too?"

"Hell no! She barely had any time for me, let alone having the free time on her calendar to hook up with another guy."

"So, you see, now I'm getting confused," Ethan said, referring to his notes once more. "Because yesterday you told me your relationship with Ms. Hart was *'completely strong. Bulletproof strong.'*"

"And it was."

"And yet you were having an affair with her best friend."

"I'd hardly call it that."

"What would you call it?"

"Lily and I, we have a connection. We like each other's company. We spend time together because our lives are very similar."

"In what way?"

"Well, let's see. Lily has been in Elena's shadow ever since they both broke into the industry, and me? Well, I've been in that same shade, only being allowed to speak when I'm spoken to and never being allowed to challenge the lifestyle."

"A lifestyle that meant you had a pretty comfortable standard of living."

"I earn my own money, Detective. We also went through that yesterday, remember?"

Ethan nodded, watching as the ego-fueled entrepreneur preened himself like an expensive Persian cat. He fought to hide his contempt for the man. He was never in love with Elena Hart. In fact, Ethan doubted he'd loved anybody except himself. What's more, the guy had a much different take on his affair with Lily Craven, which was sad, but the saddest thing of all was that Elena Hart had been oblivious to the whole thing: the lies, the deceit, the treachery. It seemed that she'd been surrounded by people who only had their own self-interests at heart and who would do anything to maintain their privileged lifestyle by staying out of jail.

Either way, somebody here was responsible for Elena Hart's murder.

***

Max Roth sat in the living quarters and glared at the interview room door. He knew his name would come up again soon. Why wouldn't it? He was one of the few people that had daily interactions with Elena Hart, and probably the person who knew her the best. He'd dragged her out of the slums of Detroit, polished and cleaned her until she'd shone like the brightest of diamonds, and introduced her to the kind of people only the most highly successful could ever dream of meeting. He had created a star in Elena Hart, a bright supernova. He had been the architect of her rise and the pillar of strength that had kept her in the public eye for over half a decade. Without him, she would have still been waiting tables in dive bars, getting her ass slapped and her tits felt on a nightly basis.

And yet she'd been looking to replace him. That was the word on the street, a series of coincidental rumors and whisperings that suggested his shiny diamond was looking to cut him out of the loop, replace him like a pair of worn shoes. That had made him madder than a mad hatter, had him spitting with rage and throwing whiskey glasses at the wall. How dare she? How could she even consider letting somebody else take his place when she knew better than anybody how hard he'd worked to get her there and how many hours he'd spent on the telephone, making sure she got the best assignments, the most media exposure, and the highest number of followers this side of the Atlantic.

Now she was gone, and he was in the same position he would have been in if Elena had done the unthinkable and gone through with her plan, except this way, he hadn't been replaced. This way, he kept his dignity, his position of strength, and if he kept his head straight and didn't give too much away to the sneaky-eyed detective and his cute-as-a-button partner, he would walk away from this investigation a free man, and with a chance of securing Elena Hart's ongoing image rights and maybe a highly lucrative exposé, penned by yours truly.

He smiled at that last thought. He'd always been able to spin a positive news story out of a catastrophe, and this was no exception. Max Roth was a survivor. No, more than that, he was a thriver, and in this instance, he would thrive like no other.

***

In the distance, no more than three hundred meters away from the police training facility, a group of photographers hunkered down behind a fuel silo, their collars pulled up against the bracing winds and the sub-zero temperatures. The lead reporter, Harper Mayfield, held her army issue binoculars up to her bitterly cold cheeks and watched as Detective Steele held a confrontational conversation with Elena Hart's boyfriend, James Bateman. There was no doubt in her mind: the guy was a suspect, and if his involvement was proven, it would become the story of the year, perhaps even the decade. She could see the headline now: *Jealous Boyfriend Slaughters Wealthy Supermodel During Private Jet Love Spat.*

Her boss from the Chicago Tribune had attached her to Elena Hart's trip to Churchill to try and get an interview with the world-famous model, but neither of them had expected something like this to go down. It meant she was in just the right place to report on the police investigation, a moment of good fortune she'd been due. The problem was that she wasn't the only one looking for the big scoop, and that meant she had to act fast.

She reached for her phone and dialed her boss. He was going to want to hear all about where the investigation was headed.

Chapter 5

Fractured Trust

Ethan sat in the side office, drinking coffee and running the day's interviews over and over in his head. He'd learned a lot in a short space of time, but the problem was none of it amounted to anything. Sure, Air Marshal Rodriguez had a dangerous obsession with the murder victim, and Elena's boyfriend and her best friend had been having an affair behind her back, but he had no evidence linking any of them to her death. At best, he had motive, but motive on its own wasn't enough. He needed a cause of death, and he needed something to connect one or all of these people to a conclusive piece of evidence.

Bateman was a spoiled, privileged smart-ass, and he knew how to get under Ethan's skin. He didn't like that about him. In fact, he wanted him to be guilty more than anybody else in that room, which was a problem. Ethan knew from his training under Charles Schaeffer that objectivity was one of the key weapons in tracking down a murderer. Without it, Ethan could be chasing shadows for weeks, maybe months. It was the one thing that the officers in charge of finding his fiancée's killer couldn't get into their thick skulls. They had a suspect in mind, Danny Barnes, a lowlife street criminal who had been eluding the Toronto PD for longer than any of them cared to remember, and just because he'd been seen in the vicinity of the apartment on the night Rebecca died, they'd decided, almost on day one, that it was him. They couldn't even bring themselves to consider anybody else, even though Ethan tried to tell them. Man, he'd tried. He'd even pulled together a file of evidence containing photographs, video footage, witness statements, and even a bloodied fingerprint on the handrail to the third floor. Of course, it didn't help that the guy he was convinced had killed his fiancée and had friends in high places. The highest of offices as far as the state of Ontario was concerned.

There was a tap on the door and Ethan looked up to see Emily standing there, her mask pulled down around her chin, exposing her full lips and high cheekbones.

"How you doing?" she asked, taking his coffee cup from his hands and sipping the steaming hot liquid.

"Got a lot of information, but not a lot of evidence."

"Such as?"

"Lily was sleeping with James Bateman."

"No way!" Emily raised a hand to her mouth as she tried to keep her voice down. "The boyfriend?"

"The very same."

"Man, that's motive right there. What about the Air Marshal?"

"I made a few calls after your conversation with Ms. Craven. Turns out he was madly obsessed with Elena Hart. So much so that he was almost forcefully removed from the military."

Emily shook her head. "The plot thickens."

"Yeah. You could say that. It seems like Ms. Hart's beauty inspired a whole bunch of crazy behavior. How are you getting on with the autopsy?"

"I couldn't find anything internally, no signs of organ damage or hemorrhaging, not even a bruise or a broken bone. However, I did find something that could be interesting."

"And what was that?"

"Muscle tissue damage, as if there had been some level of spasming or contraction just prior to death."

"Meaning?"

"Hard to say. I've taken some blood samples and had a courier take them downtown to the medical facility in Churchill."

It was Ethan's turn to sound excited. "I hope you put a fast-track order on them."

Emily cocked her head. "Do I look like a fresh-faced intern? Of course, they're on a fast-track order, for what it's worth. In truth, I have no idea how good the facilities are up here, but with any luck, and assuming the courier doesn't get stuck in a snowdrift on his way there, we should get them back later today."

Ethan clenched his fists, feeling the adrenaline of the chase kicking in. If they could get a handle on the thing that killed Elena Hart, they could start to put the squeeze on her entourage. So far, he'd been playing nice, but nice would only get him so far.

"Anyway," Emily said, handing back the empty coffee cup and zipping up her coat. "I'm going back to the chiller. Let me know if anything else comes up."

Ethan followed her to the door. "Likewise. And Emily?"

She turned and looked up at him. It was at times like these he could see Rebecca in her eyes and in the dimples that formed in the corners of her mouth when she smiled. It made him feel guilty for forming such a close friendship with his partner.

"We'll get to the bottom of this. I know we will."

She pinched his cheek and winked impishly. "Never in any doubt."

As she departed, Ethan was confronted by the freelance photographer.

"Mr. Bryant," he said. "You almost made me jump out of my skin."

"Sorry," Leo replied, running a hand through his foppish hair. "I just thought you might want to see this."

He handed a phone to Ethan. The screen displayed an animated newsflash, the headline of which read:

Suspect in *Murder* of *Supermodel Elena Hart, Exposed* as *Professional Con Artist*

Ethan's mouth fell open as he glared at the story. It had been written by the Post's chief reporter, Harper Mayfield, somebody he knew well from a dozen other cases. She was tenacious and dogged and was almost always first to the big story. The news flash had been posted less than five minutes ago.

"Who else knows about this?" Ethan asked.

"Well, the whole world, I guess. Or pretty soon they will."

"No," Ethan pointed toward the window. "Not out there. I mean, in here?"

Leo eyed the other passengers. "Most of them have been talking or reading, and I haven't mentioned it to anyone."

"Good. Don't." He watched as Bateman stood at the coffee machine, tapping his well-polished shoes on the floor as he hummed to himself. The guy was a world-class sleazeball, that much was certain, and if this story was to be believed, he was also a lowlife conman. "Thanks for bringing this to me. I appreciate it."

"Hey, no problem. Whatever helps get this thing resolved as soon as possible. You know, we all want to get out of here and go home."

"And you will," Ethan replied, grabbing his notepad. "I promise. Hey, Mr. Bateman? I need a few more minutes of your time if you don't mind."

The guy's eyes widened with shock. "What, now?"

"That's correct." Ethan opened the interview room door. "Right now."

***

"Looks like some people out there have been able to find some things out about you that you haven't revealed to us." Ethan tossed his phone onto the table and watched James's face drop. "Some very interesting things. You care to comment?"

"No, I don't," James replied, folding his arms. "Because it bears no relevance to the things you're investigating."

"You mean, you think that being a con artist living under an alias and worming your way into a life of luxury under false pretenses isn't relevant to the police? Tell me, Mr. Bateman, how do you come to that conclusion?"

James pushed the phone away. "So what? A lot of people do it."

"Do they?"

"You'd be surprised. Do you think I was happy living in a one-bedroom apartment, working three jobs to pay the bills? You think I wanted to live the rest of my life doing meaningless work for people who could barely look me in the eye?"

"So you decided to build a fake life for yourself and somehow convince one of the world's most glamorous figures to fall in love with you."

"It wasn't easy."

"I can imagine."

"No, you can't. Nobody can. It takes a lot of planning, a lot of soul searching, and a whole bunch of sacrifice to pull something like this off. I was Aaron Tamkin from Iowa, a nobody with no education, no prospects, and a family that could care less. I was fed up eating from a can, watching as kids I went to school with rode around in fast cars and designer clothing, looking at me as if I was something they'd found stuck to the bottom of their two hundred dollar sneakers."

"So how did you do it?"

James closed his eyes and rubbed his temples. All of a sudden, he didn't look like the boyfriend of a wealthy glamor model. He seemed completely out of his depth, a shell of the man who had walked into the lodge just twenty-four hours ago.

"I met someone. I was drinking in a bar, wallowing in my own self-pity, drinking the cheapest whiskey I could find when this guy offered to buy me another, except he was offering the top-shelf stuff."

"Sounds like you found yourself a friend."

"That wasn't what I thought at the time. I thought the guy was a creep in his cotton jacket, necktie, and tailored slacks. I told him I only got wasted alone and to get lost, but he was persistent, and eventually, I relented. After that, we sat there all night talking. He told me I looked like a guy who needed a helping hand, and I told him that was probably about right. He said he'd been in my shoes a few years back, not knowing which way to turn or how to pay next month's rent, but that eventually, he figured he had a calling, and it was that moment of clarity that turned his life around."

"And what was this life-changing event?"

"He found out he could convince people to do things they didn't want to do just by pretending to be something he wasn't. Once he'd figured that out, he quit his job flipping burgers and flipped people instead. He spent a month pretending to be an insurance salesman and sold three large fake policies, earning himself over thirty thousand bucks. After that, he got into real estate and convinced an elderly couple to sell him their home for a stake in a Las Vegas casino that didn't exist. After they left, he flipped the property on to the next buyer and walked away with four hundred thousand big ones."

"Sounds like this guy had no morals."

"Guy didn't need any. He was pulling in more green than I could earn in twenty years." James seemed energized once more. "I knew I had to get in on it, so I asked him to train me."

"And did he?"

He nodded, grinning. "In six months, I'd convinced a guy that my fake Rolex was real and sold it to him for ten thousand bucks. Then, I convinced a young woman to give me the keys to her Porsche 911 Carrera after I told her it was stolen and had to be impounded. After that, I tricked my way onto an all-expenses-paid cruise around the Caribbean."

"All because this guy told you you could."

James shook his head. "Because he showed me how."

"And how did you convince these people to believe these incredible lies?"

"Confidence," he replied, smirking. "It's all in the tell. Doesn't matter what you say. What matters is the way you say it. You have to believe what you're telling them, even if it's the biggest crock you've ever told. If you believe it, and you say it like you really believe it, then most of the time, they'll believe it too, particularly if you pick the right target."

"Target?" Ethan said, feeling his blood begin to simmer. "You make it sound like these people aren't real human beings with real frailties and real emotions."

"Well, you see, that's the best part. You have to select your target based on a little background research. The guy who bought the Rolex was trying to bag a big job in the city. The girl with the Porsche had already been cautioned by the police for a DUI. And the cruise? Well, let's just say the sweetheart who gave me the free pass was open to a good-looking sweet talker in a nice suit."

"So, you manipulate people based on what you find out about them?"

James cocked his finger and winked. "You got it."

"And what about Elena? What was her weakness?"

The question seemed to stun James, and he slowly ran a hand across his eyes.

"I guess you don't want to answer that one," Ethan said, reading the room, "because you're ashamed."

"You don't get it," James said. "You would never understand."

"Why don't you try me?"

James glanced at the water dispenser. "Can I get a drink?"

"Sure." Ethan filled a paper cup and placed it in front of him. "Now, about Elena?"

"She'd been in a whole series of relationships before me. You probably read about them in the press. Hollywood actors, pop stars, millionaires. Every single relationship ended in disaster, and each time, Elena was painted to be some sort of diva, a woman who sulked if she didn't get what she wanted and threw a tantrum if things weren't up to her standards." He sipped his water. "Which was bullshit, by the way. Elena was the sweetest person I'd ever met. So kind, so funny."

Ethan decided not to point out that despite all of that, James had decided to sleep with Elena Hart's best friend behind her back.

"I decided to gatecrash one of her society events and picked the name, James Bateman, using the social media profile of a guy who had recently died to build my back story—successful nightclub owner, self-made man."

"And she bought it?"

"Why wouldn't she? I knew that Elena wasn't looking for love, so I offered to be a friend, accompanying her on shoots and being her dinner date, but never pushing the idea of romance. She'd been burned so many times before I figured I'd be shot down in flames if I made a move too soon. She liked that. She appreciated me not coming on too strong, but little by little, day by day, those feelings began to grow."

"So, you tricked her into falling in love with you. How do you feel about that now that she's lying in there on a cold, metal table."

"That had nothing to do with me!" James yelled, standing and slamming his hands down. "No matter what my intentions were initially, I loved Elena."

Ethan set down his pen and tried to speak as calmly as possible. "Mr. Bateman, or should I call you Mr. Tamkin? Might I suggest you calm down and take a seat."

The conman glared at him; his cheeks flushed. "The name's James Bateman. Aaron Tamkin died a long time ago."

As he sat down, Ethan checked his notes. "So, let me get this straight. You lied to Ms. Hunt about who you were, convincing her to fall in love with you so that you had access to her money, and then began an affair with her friend and makeup artist, Lily Craven—an affair which was ongoing at the time of Ms. Hunt's untimely demise."

James didn't reply.

"Now, what kind of picture do you think that paints for us, Mr. Bateman?" Ethan continued. "The picture of a grieving partner? A man who would do anything for the woman he loved?"

James placed his head in his hands. "I know how it looks, but you have to believe me. I thought the world of Elena. It's true, Lily and I had spoken about running away together, and who knows, perhaps we would have gone through with it, but that didn't mean I didn't love Elena, too. She was my best friend; somebody I would have protected with my life."

Ethan eyed the con artist, not knowing whether he could believe a single word that came out of his mouth. He'd lied to them about his relationship with Elena, he'd lied to them about earning his own money, and now the guy was alleging he still loved his girlfriend, even though Lily had told Ethan their relationship had been killing him.

One thing was for certain. It didn't matter whether James Bateman would lay down his life for Elena Hunt because somebody had gotten to her first and left Ethan with a riddle to solve. And solve it he would. He just needed more time.

***

Ethan decided to talk to Lily again, even though he knew his request would be unpopular. Since he'd revealed to her that he knew about the affair, her body language had altered substantially. She appeared jittery and unsure of herself, her eyes flitting from person to person as if she were looking for someone to help her.

"What do you know about James Bateman's businesses, Ms. Craven?" Ethan asked as they sat in the interview room.

Lily shrugged and picked at a nail. Ethan noticed that the polish was looking chipped and ragged. "We don't talk about it much."

"But he's a wealthy entrepreneur with a string of clubs. Surely, that comes up in conversation."

"Maybe a few times, but mainly, we just talk about our future together. You know, at one point, we were planning to leave town together, make our own way in life, away from the modeling industry and everything that surrounds it."

Ethan made another note. At least that part of her story backed up what Bateman had told him.

"So, you never visited one of his clubs or wondered where he was going when he headed out on business trips?"

She laughed. "His business trips were all bullshit. When he told Elena he was traveling to check out a new potential venue, he was spending the weekend with me in Miami or Los Angeles."

She seemed a little too proud of the lie for Ethan's liking. If Lily Craven was Elena Hart's best friend, she was doing a heck of a job hiding it.

"So, he never went to see these clubs or meet with any new clients?"

She shook her head. "He had a manager who dealt with all of that for him. A guy named Paul Leblanc. James said he trusted Paul to ensure things ran smoothly while he sat back and enjoyed the profits."

"And that never seemed odd to you?"

Lily shrugged, but behind her eyes, the wheels were starting to turn. "Should it?"

"You tell me, Ms. Craven. You know the guy a hell of a lot better than I do."

She picked at the nail again, this time tearing a loose piece of polish from her cuticle. "Now that you mention it, he said he had a club in Indianapolis, but I never saw it when we were there."

Ethan let out a long sigh. "Lily, I'm going to tell you something now that will be upsetting for you, but if I don't, there's every chance you'll see it on your news feed later today, and I can assure you, finding out that way will be so much worse."

She looked up at him, tears beginning to well in her eyes. She looked like she was lost, as if the events of the past two days were slowly snowballing around her, burying her under an avalanche she just couldn't escape.

Ethan placed his hands on the table and took a breath. "It's about James."

***

Emily stood in the cold confines of the lab and set down her scalpel. She'd almost completed her investigations into the cause of Elena Hart's death, and so far, she'd found nothing concrete. She only hoped the blood tests came back with something conclusive, something that gave both her and Ethan a foothold in what was becoming an increasingly frustrating case.

Ethan had filled her in on the news of James Bateman's real identity, Aaron Tamkin, and while Emily was shocked, it still didn't lead them to a solution to the case. Sure, on paper the guy looked as guilty as a thief with his hands in the family vault, but unless they could link him to a piece of hard evidence that would convince a jury he was the one to stick the needle in Elena Hart's neck, their motive was worthless.

She stood back and blew out cold air. The starkness of the surroundings was starting to get to her. The ground outside was permanently covered in thick ice and a deep layer of snow, and the sky was as gray as concrete. Sure, the tundra was a site to behold, but she longed for some warmth, some sunshine, and perhaps a few trees and a little grass to push her toes into. The whole environment was making her feel closed in and claustrophobic.

The only thing that brightened her day was her check-ins with Ethan. He was fun to be around—he always had been, in spite of the tragedy he'd had to live through. She'd done what she could to help him deal with it, even though it had happened a long time before the pair of them had met, but it was always right there, never far away. She could empathize with his emotions. She understood grief more than anyone. She'd lost her sister to cancer when they were both in their teens, and it had knocked the wind out of her for what had seemed like forever. She still missed Ronie. She knew that feeling of loss would never fade, and she didn't want it to.

She'd grown closer to Ethan since the chief had partnered her up with the newly appointed detective on the case of the Montreal Butcher. It was the first time Emily had seen the barbaric nature of humanity up close, and it had affected her more than she'd expected. Ethan had seen that, even before she'd realized it herself, and rather than tell her to 'man up' like so many other male officers in his position would have, he gave her space. He suggested things to her, rather than imposing his views, letting her know that, in his experience, the best way to deal with trauma was to give the mind time to process everything. She respected him for that. He was a good guy. He was the one who had suggested she take the criminal justice exams, and undergo major investigations training. Because of that, she was one of the few medical examiners on the force who could double as a junior detective. She could never thank him enough for his faith in her.

The problem was that no matter how easygoing Ethan was, he needed results, and she was letting him down. Their whole case was hanging on the blood tests, coming back with something they could use, and right now, everything was on ice in more ways than one.

***

Ethan Steele stood on the front porch, his hood pulled down against the icy chill. The storm was starting to build out there, and at some point, there was going to be a snow dump like no other. He could feel the sub-zero temperatures against his cheeks and forehead, the freezing oxygen filling his lungs with ice. It wasn't the only thing he was worried about. Things were moving at a snail's pace, so slow they were almost going in reverse. The lack of speed was harming his investigation.

The press seemed to be one step ahead of them, firing misguided information off into the stratosphere without a second's hesitation, creating a social media frenzy that was making him and Emily look like a couple of amateurs. He knew the reporters were out there watching them, the photographers with their high definition, ultra zoom cameras. Pretty soon, the whole place was going to be buzzing with the world's media, everyone so hungry for information, exclusive images, and case-defining soundbites. He had to do something to stop it before everything got out of control, but he knew the only way he could sate their hunger was to feed them something meaty. The problem was, he didn't have anything—not really.

With news of James Bateman's true identity out there, the world was already forming an opinion on who killed Elena Hart. Before any evidence had been presented or anybody had been put before a jury, the court of public opinion was identifying their man and deciding exactly what had gone down in the glamorous model's final moments. That wasn't fair to her, and it wasn't helpful to their case.

One way or another, he was going to get to the truth, and if it meant he had to bang a few heads together to get to it, then that's what he would do. It was time for the nice guy mask to be set aside and for the real investigation to start—beginning with the Air Marshal and his obsession. If anybody knew what had happened in that cabin, it was the guy who was tasked with protecting Elena Hart. The guy who had failed.

Chapter 6

Beneath the Ice

Rodriguez sat with his arms folded and his back straight, furiously chewing a stick of gum as if it were his last meal. Ethan glared at him unblinking, letting the silence fill the vacuum between them. The Air Marshal knew something. Ethan knew he did. He just had to figure out a way of prizing it from him.

"You going to ask me some questions, or what?" he said.

"Depends if you've got something to say."

"Well, you dragged me back in here, so I'm guessing you think I know something I haven't told you yet?"

"And do you?"

Rodriguez shook his head. "I said everything I had to say yesterday. And anyway, shouldn't you be talking to the boyfriend? We've all seen the news, and we heard the argument he and that makeup artist had earlier today. I'm guessing those two were more than just buddies."

Ethan tried to hide his disappointment. He should have known the others would be talking. There was no way he and Emily could keep a lid on everything. "Tell me about that," he said, trying to use the news to his advantage. "Did you sense anything on the plane, like a tension between Lily Craven and Elena Hart?"

"No. I only met Lily on board, and Elena was pretty out of it for most of the flight."

"How about Mr. Bateman? Did he seem distracted at all? How was the conversation between him and Ms. Hart? Any crosswords?"

"That's a lot of questions," Rodriguez answered. "And how the hell should I know?"

"Because your role was to look out for your client, and the best way to do that is to observe and listen. I assume they teach you that at Air Marshal school, or wherever it is people like you get trained."

Rodriguez barely flinched at the barbed comment. "I observed. I observed a lot more than any of them knew."

"Such as?"

"Such as the tension between the freelance photographer and the stylist. Such as the bitterness Elena's documentarian clearly felt toward her. And such as the way her agent kept watching her as if he wanted to tell her something but was too afraid to say." He sipped his coffee and eyed Ethan. "There were a lot of secrets on that airplane, detective, and not a lot of love."

"And why do you think that is?"

"Because not one of them truly liked Elena. I mean, they may have said they did—they'd fawned over her as if she were some sort of queen—but deep down, they were all just feeding on the carcass, taking what they could until her bones were picked clean."

"And who do you think was the instigator of that?"

"Max Roth, James Bateman, Sarah Locke, you name it. Every single one of them wanted a piece of her. She was the goose that was laying the golden eggs, and they were up there in the clouds, stealing the gold from right under her nose. You've got to realize that without Elena, these people were nothing. Roth only had mediocre D-list celebrities on his books, Bateman was a conman who was kidding his way through life, Sarah Locke was an intern at a media company until Elena picked her out of obscurity, and Tom Oates had been kicked off a multi-million dollar project because of his screw up of a partner. Elena rescued them all from that and gave them a life none of them could afford, and not one of them truly deserved."

"And what about Lily Craven? Where did she fit in all of this?"

Rodriguez took another sip of his coffee. "She was fucking Elena's boyfriend, so you tell me."

His forthrightness surprised Ethan. After the first interview, during which the ex-soldier had been on the defensive, he was now saying things that seemed like he wanted to get out into the open.

"And did you see anything to suggest that any one of those people were planning to harm Ms. Hart in any way?"

"If I had, Detective, don't you think I would have intervened? I mean, that was what I was there for, after all. You made a point of reminding me of that yesterday."

Ethan stood and grabbed a cup of water from the dispenser. Despite his openness, the detective still felt something bugging him about the Air Marshal's presence on the plane.

"I checked back through Elena Hart's previous assignments. It was very rare for her to travel with a security detail. Why do you think she did so this time? Was there something about this trip that had unnerved her? I mean, it's not like she was traveling to a war zone or a dangerous part of the world."

Rodriguez shrugged. "I just take the jobs my boss assigns me."

"But that's not true, is it? We already know about your obsession with Ms. Hart, and I also know, from talking to your superior officer, Captain Sissons, that you raised your hand for this assignment, practically begging him to put your name on the roster."

Rodriguez's eye shifted a little. "There were three possible jobs, and this one was the most challenging. I don't take easy assignments. They bore me."

"So it's coincidental that this one included the one person you'd been obsessing over since your time in the army."

"I think obsession is a strong word. I was a fan. Still am. As far as I'm aware, that's not a crime."

"No, but murder is."

"Are you accusing me, Detective?"

"I'm just stating the facts."

Rodriguez glared out the window. "If you have something on me, tell me"

"That implies there's something to have."

"And that comment tells me you don't have a damn thing. Look, I know you, and I got off on the wrong foot, what with me criticizing your civilian background and all, but I'm on your side here. I want the bastard who killed Elena Hart caught more than anybody because whoever did it made me look like I'm bad at my job. Which I'm not. I'm a damn good Air Marshal with an impeccable record. Just ask the captain."

Ethan knew he was right. He'd spoken to his captain about Rodriguez's performance since he'd transferred from the army, and as far as Captain Sissons was concerned, he was one of the best he had. If that was true, how had the murderer been able to divert the security guard's attention away from his client long enough to inject something into the base of her skull? It just didn't make sense.

**

Harper Mayfield sat in the newly constructed media tent and read through her notes. Her editor had practically salivated at the breaking news of James Bateman's secret identity and had been even more excited about the suggestion he may have been screwing a mysterious woman behind Elena Hart's back. He'd given Harper a clear and direct instruction to use her sources to get as much dirt on the guy as possible, and write a sensationalist piece listing every one of his crimes.

She could only imagine how much her recently published newsflash had pissed Ethan Steele off. There was no doubt it had the potential to derail whatever he was doing in the training lodge, but she also suspected it could lead him to a conclusion he may have otherwise missed. It had been less than forty-eight hours since Elena Hart's death, and there was no doubt the chief of police would be putting pressure on Ethan and the doctor to bring this thing to a head. She suspected they could use whatever help they could get, and if finding information out through the kind of backdoors she was used to kicking down assisted them while also helping her get the big scoop, then everyone was a winner.

"Hey, Harps," her lead photographer, Darren Kelly, said as he devoured his third donut. "How long you think we're gonna be stuck out here in the ice-capades, waiting for something to happen?"

"As long as it takes," she replied, watching as Emily Carter walked between the buildings with what looked like a report in her hands.

"But we've already predicted the outcome of the case, right? That slimeball Bateman did it. Any idiot can see that."

"We're not employed to jump to conclusions, Darren. We're employed to present our findings in a way that will engage the reader."

"And you found something those imbeciles in that lodge didn't even see coming. Maybe you should work for the police, Harps. You'd save Toronto PD a whole bunch of green."

She let the photographer's clumsy attempt at a complement hang in the air and thought about her next step. The one thing she didn't know, the thing that she really wanted to find out before any other reporter, was how Elena Hart was killed. She needed that even more than she needed a warmer coat or a pair of snow shoes.

As Harper watched Emily Carter enter the building, closing the door behind her, she decided to make the call. She had friends in important places, after all, and she knew this particular friend would have just what she was looking for.

***

There was a tap at the door, and Ethan looked up. Emily was standing there. "Ethan, do you have a minute?"

"I'm just in the middle of an interview here. Can it wait?"

Emily shook her head. "I'm afraid not, and I think you're going to want to hear this."

He paused the recording and gestured for Rodriguez to head back into the living quarters. "I'm sorry about this," he said. "Hopefully, I won't be too long."

"No problem," Rodriguez replied, stepping out into the hall and tossing his Styrofoam cup into the trash. "Take your time. It's not like any of us are going anywhere."

Emily took a seat as Ethan set aside his notes. He was a little annoyed but he chose not to show it. He'd felt he had been getting somewhere with the interview, and now he knew he would have to build up the rapport from the start once again.

"I hope this is good," he said.

"Oh, it's good." Emily threw a report onto the table.

"What's this?"

"It's from the lab at Churchill. They ran the tests."

"On the blood samples?"

"The very same."

Ethan picked up the papers and scanned through them. Aside from a few paragraphs of jargon, he had no idea what he was looking at.

"Okay, you're going to have to translate this for me."

Emily grinned and folded her arms. "Tetrodotoxin."

"I have no idea what that is."

"No, most people don't. You're unlikely to come into contact with it during everyday life."

"You want to fill me in?"

"Tetrodotoxin is a neurotoxin that's extracted from pufferfish, porcupinefish, triggerfish, and other similar marine animals. It's used as a defense mechanism to ward off predators, attacking the nerve tissue of the subject, effectively paralyzing them."

"Okay, but how would something that exists inside marine creatures find its way into Elena Hart's bloodstream, and even if it did, could it kill her?"

"In a big enough dose, yes. After injection, the neurotoxin would get to work on the nerve tissue, causing the contraction I saw in Ms. Hart's muscle tissue, but worse than that, in extreme cases, it can cause respiratory problems."

"Meaning she could have literally stopped breathing."

"After an initial period of paralysis, yes."

Ethan felt his excitement build. They'd been looking for a smoking gun, and this one was practically on fire.

"So, you think somebody smuggled this stuff on board and injected it into Elena Hart while she was sleeping?"

Emily nodded. "She wouldn't even have felt anything. If administered correctly, it would have paralyzed her before suffocating her. As death's go, it would be almost painless."

Ethan re-read the notes. "But this report says Tetrodotoxin is not widely distributed amongst the scientific community, meaning that—"

"—that whoever caused that puncture wound had to have some high-level access to a regulated chemical."

Immediately, Ethan thought of his discussion with Lieutenant Murray of the 38th Infantry Division. If anyone was going to have access to a highly toxic substance used by the US Army, it would be the guy who had just left the military.

"I think I need to talk to Air Marshal Rodriguez again," he said, opening the door. "And this time, Emily, I want you to listen in."

***

"Tetrodotoxin," Ethan said, slamming the report down on the table as Rodriguez took his seat.

"I'm sorry?"

"You heard me, Air Marshal. Tetrodotoxin, a neurotoxin that the doctor here says can be lethal, given the right dosage."

"I'm sure you're right," Rodriguez replied. "But I have no idea what that has to do with me."

Ethan glared at him, looking for any sort of tell. Rodriguez's expression was impassive. If he was lying, he was doing a damn good job of it.

"You've met the doctor, I assume," Ethan said, signaling for Emily to introduce herself.

"Doctor Emily Carter," she said. "I was brought here to examine Ms. Hart's body, as well as other things."

"And a good job, too," Rodriguez replied. "The sooner we can find out what killed her, the sooner you can find the killer, right?"

"Right," Ethan replied. "Which is why this discovery is extremely important. You see, Tetrodotoxin was found in Ms. Hart's bloodstream and in a volume that was almost certain to have stopped her breathing."

The Air Marshal's face turned ashen. "She was injected?"

Ethan nodded. "Somebody decided to kill Elena Hart on that plane, Air Marshal, and the fact they used this neurotoxin means it was premeditated. Somebody wanted her out of the picture badly enough to risk being caught on an airplane full of Ms. Hart's nearest and dearest."

Ethan let the room fall silent, waiting for Rodriguez to reveal something. He had to be the one who obtained the neurotoxin. He just had to be.

"I'm guessing you think I was able to get this stuff because of my military background," he said.

"That's what we're here to ask you," Ethan replied.

"And I'm telling you, it wasn't me."

"It's unlikely anybody else on that plane could have gotten their hands on it without some sort of help from somebody with the right contacts," Emily replied. "Even though this toxin is created naturally, it needs processing and refinement to get it to the strength and consistency that's damaging to humans. Refined Tetrodotoxin isn't made freely available to the public for obvious reasons."

"Be that as it may, Doctor, you're talking to the wrong guy. Even if I could get my hands on the stuff, why would I want to kill Elena Hart?"

"Because you were obsessed with her," Ethan said, "And maybe, just maybe, she rejected your unwanted advances."

"What advances? You think I made a move on her? And when do you suppose this little event happened? While we were on the plane? In front of everyone?"

"Maybe you met up with her beforehand. Maybe you went to see her in her hotel room or intercepted her as she headed to the airport."

"Are you kidding me? I was assigned this job less than forty-eight hours before the day of the flight, Detective. I only made it to Chicago two hours before the trip. You can check that with my supervisor, or better yet, check out all the security camera footage. I'm sure you have a team scrolling through it as we speak. You may have convinced yourselves that I had a motive, but you need to prove it for it to be true."

Ethan eyed Emily, who was watching the suspect closely. They both knew Rodriguez was right. What they had was circumstantial at best. Sure, the toxin was difficult to obtain, but not impossible. Linking it to the one member of the group who had served with the military could be seen as a desperate leap on their part, and maybe, just maybe, that was exactly what it was.

They had to find something better. The question was how?

***

Harper Mayfield ended her call and glared at her phone. She couldn't believe what she'd just heard. Her contact had needed some convincing to disclose what she knew, but the money Harper's boss had agreed to pay for the big exclusive would more than compensate the lab technician for her guilty conscience. The tests had been conclusive. Tetrodotoxin, a chemical she'd come across during an investigation she'd carried out regarding the US military's alleged planned use of nerve agents in the battlefield, had been the cause of Elena Hart's death. That only served to confirm one thing—this was now a murder investigation.

Sure, Harper had run the story about Elena Hart's partner and conman, James Bateman, earlier in the day, but this new news put somebody else firmly in the frame, and he was the one person Harper suspected all along. The guy with years of military training and the one guy who had been hastily rushed onto the job just hours before the flight had left Chicago.

She started typing immediately, drafting a headline she knew would get more than a million hits and make the world sit up and pay attention.

It's Confirmed—Glamorous Supermodel Poisoned. Is The Air Marshal Hired to Keep Elena Hart Safe Guilty Of Her Murder?

***

Emily sat in the office and watched as Ethan made notes. It had been a long day. They were both exhausted. They had learned a lot, but it still felt like they were no closer to the truth. James and Lily had confessed to their affair just prior to Elena's partner being exposed as a conman. On top of that, they'd learned that Air Marshal Rodriguez had been obsessed with the supermodel, and they suspected he had access to the neurotoxin they now knew was used to kill her. All these things together amounted to a lot, but they also amounted to nothing at all. Not without something to connect the dots.

Ethan had ordered a second search of the airplane, asking the search team to look for a needle or a sharp implement of some sort that may have been used to inject Elena Hart and that might also contain traces of the regulated chemical. He'd also searched everybody in the lodge again, hoping to find something in their possession that might incriminate them. So far, they'd come up with nothing.

"Hey," Emily said, pointing at the clock. "It's late. Why don't we call it a night."

"Not until I have everything in my head written down."

"It will still be there tomorrow."

"But the mind has a habit of remembering things much clearer when you commit them to paper."

Emily liked that about her partner. He was meticulous in his approach, and he wasn't afraid of putting in the long hours. The loss of his fiancée had sparked something in him—the desire to bring every criminal he investigated to justice, even if it meant personal sacrifices had to be made. His approach inspired Emily and drove her to work just as hard. That was why they were a good team. They learned from each other.

"I'll grab us some food," she said, standing. "You need to eat."

"I'm okay. I'll probably eat some Cheetos or something before I turn in."

"Ethan, there's no way I'm letting your heart go through that. I'm making you something more nutritious."

"Like what?"

Emily shrugged. "Burritos?"

"If you can rustle something together from whatever's in the refrigerator, go ahead."

She let the door slowly close behind her as she eyed the room. The passengers all looked as tired as she felt, and who could blame them? They'd been holed up in the lodge for two days with no access to the outside world except via their phones, and all of them had been banned from sending messages. It was an isolating experience, with the weather outside deteriorating by the second. If the forecast was to be believed, they could be snowed in within a day. The thought sent chills through Emily's body. If they were to get out of there before things started to go crazy, they needed to move fast.

"Hey, Dr. Carter, is it?" Sarah Locke appeared out of nowhere, her normally pristine hair hanging limply against her pale complexion.

"It is. And you're Sarah, Elena's project manager."

"Ex-project manager," Sarah replied. "Sorry, did that sound too crass?"

"Not at all. What can I do for you, Ms. Locke?"

"I need to get out of here. This has been going on way longer than I expected, than any of us expected, and I have things I have to get back to, people who will be expecting me."

"But weren't you planning on being in Churchill for four nights as part of the magazine's photo shoot? Why would people back home be expecting you?"

The project manager's eyes darted anxiously toward the other passengers. "It was a turn of phrase. I didn't mean it the way it sounded. I just...I just can't be here any longer. It's getting to me, you know. I suffer from claustrophobia, and this place is just...it's just so closed in. I feel like I can't breathe around these people."

Emily watched as the young woman's expression changed. She appeared on the verge of tears. "Look. I know this isn't an ideal situation, but we all have to pull together to make sure we find out what happened to Elena. If you leave, then everybody will start to leave, and the chances of us ever figuring out what went on up there will rapidly diminish. I just ask you to stay with us for a little while longer while we conclude our investigation."

"And how long will that take?" Sarah asked, her voice rising in pitch. "A few hours? A few days? A week?"

"I'm afraid I can't say."

"So it could be that long, right? A week? Maybe longer?"

"Are you afraid of something here, Ms. Locke?" Emily asked, leading her to a quieter part of the lodge, away from prying eyes. "Is there something you want to tell me?"

"No...I..." she paused, looking around the room, seemingly searching for cameras or recording devices.

"Look," Emily said. "We know you were the one to bring Rodriguez on board, and we know the two of you hooked up."

"Barely," Sarah scoffed. "We made out after a few drinks in the back of a cab. Hey, I'm not proud of it, but I'm a single woman, and I take what I can get. Anyway, Mike's a nice guy. How was I to know all this would happen while he wasn't looking?"

"But you thought that qualified him for the job?"

"What? No? I called the agency, and he was the one they sent. It was just a coincidence."

Emily could see Sarah was struggling, but she pushed on. "So why the rush to get out of here?"

"It's just...well, you haven't asked to interview me yet, and I...well, you're going to find this out eventually anyway, but Elena and I, we didn't have the best relationship."

Emily fought to control her reaction. "What do you mean by that?"

"Just that. Elena respected me as a professional because I'm reliable and I work hard, but our friendship was complicated."

"Complicated? How?"

"We were like sisters."

"So, you were friends?"

"Maybe, but friends don't always get along, do they? And Elena and me, we were like that."

Emily thought for a second. "Are you telling me you and Ms. Hart had a difficult relationship?"

Sarah offered a curt nod of acknowledgment. "It's no secret I had aspirations to be a successful supermodel. I even did some shoots, but for some reason, my career never took off like Elena's did. I guess I resented her for that in some small way, and I think Elena knew that. I know I can be a cold bitch, it's one of the things that makes me so damn good at my job, but I think the way I acted got under Elena's skin. We would argue, sometimes fight."

"Fight? You mean violently?"

"I think Elena slapped me once, and I may have shoved her." She tucked a strand of blond hair behind her ear. "But I didn't kill her if that's what you're thinking."

Emily considered the possibility. She and Ethan hadn't even considered Sarah Locke in their investigation, but with this new revelation, she thought they might have to reconsider their options.

"Detective Steele will want to talk to you about that," she said.

"Why?" Sarah seemed startled. "I've just told you everything. I just... didn't want you to find out from anybody else."

"What the hell?" Max Roth yelled from the other room. "Have you seen this? Have you seen what these damn bloodhounds have released now?"

Emily pushed past Sarah and headed into the living quarters. Everyone was gathered around the agent's cell phone, eager to see what had caused such a loud reaction.

"I have no idea what Tetrodotoxin is," James said.

"Sounds like a puzzle word," Leo Bryant replied, laughing.

"No, look, it says here," Samantha Mitchell chimed in. "It's a restricted chemical. A toxin."

"So, it was used to kill Elena?" Tom Oates asked. "But I was there the whole time. How could that have even happened?"

"Yes, but you weren't the only one in that cabin when the toxin was administered," James said. "Somebody else was in there with you, weren't they?"

All eyes turned to the Air Marshal, who was the only one who hadn't gotten up from his seat. He glared at the others defiantly, daring them to say something.

Emily looked at Ethan, who was standing in the doorway, his arms folded, shaking his head. They shared a knowing glance. There was no doubt about it. They had a leak.

Chapter 7

Toxic Evidence

Ethan was the first to rise the next day, wiping the sleep from his eyes as he made himself a coffee. The sun had barely risen, and what little light made it through the thick cloud was reflecting off the snow on the ground. There had been a storm during the night, and the tundra was now two feet deep in a white blanket. In the distance, Ethan could see the media tent. He'd been lucky that only a few of them had made it this far, but he knew more were on their way. If the weather didn't hold them off, pretty soon, there would be tens of them out there, maybe a hundred.

He watched as the brown liquid slowly filled the coffee pot, pondering last night's discovery. Somebody had leaked the presence of Tetrodotoxin in Elena Hart's bloodstream, which meant Churchill's PD was compromised. That was worrying to him. It meant that everything they did, every lead they chased down, had to be kept between himself, Emily, and the chief. That was going to make things difficult and would slow down their progress. They'd been using the local PD to scour through the security camera feeds, chase down intel on each one of the passengers, and feed back information from the second airplane search. Another leak could severely hamper the integrity of their efforts and potentially lead to a mistrial. Whatever happened, they were going to have to play it carefully from now on.

Emily had disclosed her conversation with Sarah Locke as they ate an unconventional dinner of salami burritos and potato chips that night. The news was a shock to Ethan. Sarah Locke seemed like the ultra professional, doing everything Elena Hart asked with crisp precision and machine-like efficiency. Nobody had even mentioned their fractious relationship, which meant Sarah had done an equally proficient job of keeping it under wraps. That worried him, too. If she was this good at keeping things secret, what else was she hiding from them? Sure, she volunteered the details of her fights with her boss, but that could be a double bluff, trying to throw them off the scent. He still didn't know what to make of it and was less sure about what to do.

For now, he still considered Air Marshal Rodriguez his primary suspect, and unless they uncovered something to disprove that, he intended to push the guy hard at the next interview. He was keeping something from them—Ethan could sense it—but so far, he hadn't reacted to any of the questions. That meant he was going to have to try something to unnerve Rodriguez. Something the man wouldn't be expecting.

He sat there, thinking about Rebecca, trying to imagine what she would tell him to do in this situation. She had been such a strong presence in his life, such a rock. He hadn't been a detective then. He'd been working in a corporate job, sitting at a desk every day, answering calls, filling in spreadsheets while focusing on building a future for the two of them. When she'd died, it had completely shaken his belief system and made him feel like nothing was worth it. The money they'd saved, the house they'd bought, the family they wanted. Every night, they'd sat in bed, talking about their dreams, making plans that would never come to fruition, building a future that would later be torn apart. What had been the point? Rebecca had been everything to him, the ground he walked on, the air he breathed. It had taken him so long to pull himself out of that dark, cavernous hole, and Emily had been a big part of bringing him back to reality. Their friendship had partially filled the space left by Rebecca, although it could never truly make it whole. Nevertheless, he would never forget what the doctor had done for him, and despite feeling guilty about the friendship that had blossomed between them, he knew if Rebecca was still here, she and Emily would be friends, too. They were alike: strong, intelligent, and funny. Whatever advice she gave to him, he knew it would be the same advice Rebecca would have provided. And Emily's guidance was loud and clear. Put pressure on the Air Marshal and watch how the others react.

So that was exactly what he was going to do.

***

Emily stood outside on the porch, her coat pulled around her, watching as the snow started to build up around the lodge. They were in a winter wonderland, surrounded by a rolling white wilderness, and in another life, it would be the most magical experience, like all her Christmases rolled into one, filled with spectacular scenery and a location reminiscent of Santa's North Pole. She tried not to think about the dangers posed by the roaming polar bears.

The other complication was that, inside the lodge, they had at least eight potential suspects in a murder investigation, none of whom wanted to be there, and all of whom were denying any involvement. What made the whole situation more sinister was that just across the walkway, lying in a cold room with a blanket draped over her body, was the cold corpse of Elena Hart, a woman who had once had the world at her fingertips and millions of followers around the globe idolizing her. It was a tragedy of epic proportions, a TV show with the saddest of endings.

She thought about Ethan and the cases they had worked together. There was no doubt they made a good team, but she couldn't help but feel their closeness was starting to cloud their ability to see the obvious. She knew he would never get over the loss of his fiancée, and she would never expect him to, but she also knew that their friendship was more than just the bond of two colleagues. It was like they were symbiotic, able to predict what the other person was thinking. Was their bond stopping them from seeing a different perspective or noticing things that were right in front of them?

Sometimes, at night, she would sit up in her bed and watch Ethan sleeping from across the room, wondering what he was dreaming and wondering whether she was featured in those dreams. She knew it was crazy. Why would her co-worker be dreaming about her? It was more likely he was dreaming about being with his fiancée, doing things that people in love did. She knew her feelings for her friend were purely platonic, but sometimes, she allowed herself to wonder what it would be like if they weren't. Would her emotions be reciprocated? Would Ethan think about her in the same way, or would her feelings drive him away? Was there even a remote possibility that in the future, a long way down the road, there could be affection? Love?

She shook her head, draining her coffee cup and exhaling. She always felt this way when the two of them were working together on a location. It was the isolation, the proximity. She knew she'd be fine when they headed home. She'd almost certainly be fine. She had a job to do, after all, a case to crack and a whole bunch of things to keep herself occupied.

* She and Ethan could never be more than just the best investigative team the Toronto CSIU had to offer, and she was okay with that.

Now wasn't the time to allow her emotions to get in the way of what she needed to do. And what she needed to do right now was get Air Marshal Rodriguez to crack.

***

"What do you know about Sarah Locke?" Ethan asked.

"Sarah Locke?"

"Yes. Elena's PM. Did you run any background checks before you took the assignment?"

"Sure I did," Rodriguez replied. "I'd be pretty dumb if I didn't. Everybody checked out. Sarah was reported as being the ultimate professional. In fact, she came highly recommended by some of the biggest names in the business."

"So, nothing stood out?" Emily asked. "Nothing that would suggest she could be a threat to your client?"

Rodriguez's eyes narrowed. "What are you suggesting?"

"That making out with her in the back of a cab isn't the usual way of conducting background checks."

Rodriguez grimaced. "I know that was unprofessional, but it was before I got the assignment. That doesn't mean I didn't do my job properly."

"No, it doesn't," Ethan replied. "But, you see, the thing is, we know that Ms. Locke and Ms. Hart had a longstanding friendship and that they'd worked together for many years, but we also heard a rumor that their interactions weren't always congenial."

Rodriguez shot Emily the side eye before returning his gaze to Ethan. "She has a certain way of communicating if that's what you mean. And the detail in the file suggested that the two of them could occasionally have some tense encounters, but at the time I didn't think it was a risk worth highlighting. Why? Do you?"

"We're not here to have opinions," Emily replied. "Only to gather the facts."

"It's an interesting question, though," Rodriguez said, mulling it over. "I guess it's a possibility she was involved. There were times when I wasn't in the cabin. Like when I went to the bathroom, for example."

"How many times would you say you left Ms. Hart alone?" Ethan asked.

"Maybe three times. No more than a few minutes each, but if what the press are suggesting is correct, I'm guessing that would be more than enough time to inject Ms. Hart with a deadly toxin."

Ethan made a note as Emily watched the Air Marshal adjust his position. He didn't appear entirely comfortable.

"So, knowing what you now know," she said, "you might reconsider your initial assessment of Ms. Locke as being low risk?"

"Knowing what I now know, I would say that's correct. If her relationship with Elena...Ms. Hart was as volatile as we think, then maybe I was wrong to assume the threat she posed was minimal."

"That's some admission," Ethan said. "You were supposed to be the security professional in this situation, but you're willing to concede you may have made a mistake."

"Not a mistake—I think anybody in my position would have come to the same conclusion—but hindsight is a wonderful thing, Detective. It shines a whole new light on things that, at the time, didn't seem obvious. Not to me, anyway."

"So, you don't think it's obvious to question someone who is on record as saying that she and her client often fought?"

Rodriguez took a moment to reply. "A lot of people fight. I fight with my friends all the time. Doesn't mean I want to kill them."

Ethan stood and paced the room, allowing Emily time to check her own notes.

"You say you didn't have access to Tetrodotoxin, Air Marshal. Is that right?"

"That's right. I'd never even heard of it until the press release yesterday."

"So, you've never come into contact with it before? Not even when you were stationed at the military base in Maryland? You never heard your commanding officers talking about it or came across it during your exercises?"

He shook his head. "Why would I?"

Emily shrugged. "Seems like the kind of thing someone in your position may have experienced. It's widely known that it's on the list of toxins the military have trialed."

"I wasn't involved in those trials. Never have been. Maybe I'd left the service before it was added to the list."

"Well, now, you see, that's not true, is it, Air Marshal," Ethan interjected, leaning over the table and sliding a piece of paper toward Rodriguez. "Because we checked. It was on the roster of toxins being trialed at the base in Maryland, and what's more, you were a member of the first team to deploy it in a tactical setting."

Rodriguez leaned back in his chair. "I have no idea what you're talking about."

"Oh, but we think you do," Emily said. "Because your lieutenant, the same lieutenant who told us about your relationship with your roommate, told us that not only did you help deploy the Tetrodotoxin in the field, you also volunteered to trial a non-fatal dose of it in order to assess the effects of the toxin on human nerve and muscle tissue."

Rodriguez laughed, puffing out his cheeks as he eyed them each in turn.

"Something funny, Air Marshal?"

"Oh, you guys really do your homework, don't you."

"So, you're admitting that you lied," Ethan said, his face impassive.

"There's a difference between lying, Detective, and honoring a US Military Non-Disclosure Agreement. I was told not to tell anybody, not even a federal court, so in bringing you in on what went down during what was considered highly classified activities, First Lieutenant Murray has breached that agreement."

"And you could find yourself in hot water for withholding information deemed critical in a murder investigation, Air Marshal."

Rodriguez sat there in silence, his eyes flitting, looking from Emily to Ethan, rubbing a hand across his clean-shaven chin. For just a moment, he lost his steely expression. Emily could see doubt in his eyes, a glimmer of uncertainty.

"Okay, okay," he said. "I'll come clean, but you have to understand, as soon as I saw that press release yesterday, I knew you guys would put two and two together and come up with a number that suited the story you were creating. It wasn't in my best interest to disclose what I knew."

"Not in your best interest?" Ethan exclaimed, slamming his hand on the table. "We have Elena Hart's dead body in that room, Air Marshal, her veins filled with a paralyzing toxin you had direct experience with, and you're telling me that informing us of your connection with it isn't in your best interest?"

"Because I knew you'd immediately put me in the frame for her murder."

"Well, you must be aware of how it looks."

"Oh, I'm fully aware."

"Did you kill Elena Hart?"

Rodriguez shook his head.

"Did you supply the toxin that killed Elena Hart?"

Once more, Rodriguez shook his head.

"Were you involved in a conspiracy to kill Elena Hart?"

"This is ridiculous!" Rodriguez yelled. "I'm not a murderer, Detective. I'm the guy who was hired to protect her, remember? Killing her only hurts my career! What would I gain by injecting her with a poison I knew you'd be able to link to me?"

"Maybe that's your cover! You're too obvious!"

"Believe me, I'm not that smart!"

"Or so you'd have us believe."

"Believe what you want! I had nothing to do with her death!"

Ethan started to react, but Emily held out her hands. "Okay," she said. "Why don't we all just take a minute here."

"Do I need a lawyer?" Rodriguez said. "Because I'm starting to feel like I do."

Emily shook her head. "Look, Air Marshal. We're going to take a break and discuss what we've learned, and if we have any more questions, we'll call you back. In the meantime, why don't you go back to the living quarters and think about whether there's anything else you haven't told us."

"I want her killer caught," he said, the desperation evident in his eyes. "I do. Look, I know I had a thing for Elena. Lots of guys did, but maybe my fondness could be considered an unhealthy obsession. Whatever. But I would never hurt her. Not in a million years. She was the kind of woman I dreamed of being with, the kind of woman I thought could make me happy. But hurt her? Kill her? No, that's not me. You have to believe that. You just have to."

"As I said, go grab yourself a coffee."

As Rodriguez left the room, Emily eyed her partner.

"I don't know," she said, thinking about the suspect's denial and the obvious discomfort he was in. "I really don't."

"No, me neither," Ethan replied. "Part of me says it has to be him, but something about the way he reacted. It wasn't what I expected."

He was right. They'd exposed Rodriguez's lies and linked him directly to the toxin that killed Elena Hart. In that situation, most guilty suspects would admit their involvement, but Rodriguez seemed conflicted as if he was angry that he was the only one in the room being questioned.

"So, what's next?" she asked, wondering if they were ever going to be able to leave Churchill.

Ethan looked at the door and then back at his notes. "I think it's time we spoke to Sarah Locke."

***

"Is this really necessary," Sarah said, taking a seat. "I already told Dr. Carter everything last night."

"We're just looking to fill in the blanks," Emily said. "And to understand what you told me more fully."

"There really isn't much else to say."

"Maybe. But at this stage, every little detail you can provide us might prove to be important."

Emily watched as the young project manager sat with her back straight and her hands folded, trying to look as confident as possible, but there was no denying the uncertainty behind her eyes. She was looking more and more disheveled by the hour. Her makeup was beginning to fade, and her hair hung loose around her petite face.

"If you've done nothing wrong, Ms. Locke, then you really have nothing to worry about."

"I shouldn't have told you," she replied. "About the fights Elena and I had. I shouldn't have mentioned them. You think it gives me a motive to kill her."

"Well, does it?" Ethan asked.

Sarah Locke's eyes snapped toward him. "No. It doesn't."

"But you admit yourself, you fought, often violently."

"If you classify pushing and shoving as violent, then maybe. But it didn't happen often. Two, maybe three times. We were both stubborn. That can cause tension."

"You told my colleague Elena Hart slapped you."

"Once. Yes. It wasn't hard."

"How did you react?"

"I walked away."

"So, you didn't retaliate."

"No, detective. I didn't. When things get to that point, I find the best way to diffuse the situation is to leave the room. Elena and I, our arguments were only ever short-lived. When I would come back an hour later, it was like the fight never took place."

"Was that usual?"

"Absolutely. If it wasn't, I would have quit. I can't work with people who bear grudges. Life's too damn short. Look," she said, chewing on a nail. "Do you have a cigarette? I could really use one right now."

"I didn't know you smoked," Emily said, checking her file. "We have you down as a non-smoker, occasional drinker."

"I am," Sarah replied. "That is to say, I don't smoke often. Just when I'm stressed. And right now, I'm fucking bouncing off the walls. Can you help me out or what?"

"Well, I don't smoke," Emily said, "and neither does my partner. Maybe we can find you a carton somewhere in storage, but I'm afraid it will have to wait until after this."

"And what is this, Dr. Carter? An interrogation? A witch hunt?"

"You're no witch, Sarah," Ethan said, trying to relieve the tension. "And we're not interrogating you. We're just trying to gather all the facts."

"Well then, you need to hear this. Yeah, sure, you got me. Elena and I fought. In fact, we fought a lot. I think she liked it. Her life was boring. James was boring to her, and so was her job. She wanted out. She was fed up with the endless travel and monotonous shoots. None of them meant anything to her. She wanted to do something meaningful, something that would get her noticed for the right reasons, not just because she had nice boobs and a cute ass."

"What are you saying, Ms. Locke?" Emily asked.

"Jeez, do I have to spell it out for you? Are you really that dumb? Elena was on the verge of quitting the business, of throwing the whole thing in and heading out on her own. She wanted to start a foundation for kids who needed a boost in life, you know? Help out those like her who were starting with nothing. The only thing was, there were a whole bunch of people riding on Elena's coattails, cashing in the big fat checks that she wrote them on a monthly basis."

"So, you're saying people depended on Ms. Hart."

"What I'm saying is, *no Elena, no checks*. If she quit her supermodel lifestyle, lots of people would stop getting paid, and in my experience, nothing upsets people more than when their lifestyle has to take a drastic hit."

"But why would anyone want to kill her?" Ethan asked. "If what you're saying is true, and we have no reason to doubt you, then what would anyone have to gain from Elena being permanently out of the picture?"

Sarah Locke smirked. "Ask her low-life agent about the celebrity insurance policy he took out last month. Ten million dollars and change if what I've heard is true."

Emily almost dropped her pen. She glanced at Ethan, who looked equally stunned. Emily had heard about this kind of thing but had never actually come across it in any of the cases she'd been involved with. A celebrity insurance policy was typically used by agents of the world's most famous people to protect them from the sudden death or disappearance of their most prized assets—in this case, one of the richest supermodels on the planet. If Max Roth had one of these policies, it put him squarely in the frame for her murder. How had they missed it?

"Now," Sarah said, her eyes pleading with Emily. "How about we go find that carton of cigarettes?"

***

Ethan sat in the office, wondering whether he was getting too old or whether it was the isolation dulling his usually sharp instincts. If what Sarah Locke had told them was true, they'd missed something pretty huge when pulling together the data associated with Elena Hart's entourage.

Max Locke was a sleazeball and a manipulative one at that, but other than a personality disorder the size of a large asteroid, they'd found nothing on him. Now this? What else had they missed?

Sarah Locke was a fireball of energy and as upfront as a Hummer with no steering, but she was no killer. He would bet his career on that. She had nothing to gain from telling them about her fiery relationship with Elena Hart, and what's more, she didn't give off any 'bullshit vibes.' Despite what they'd learned, he was ruling her out of the investigation. He had to focus on the facts, and the facts led them somewhere else entirely.

Rodriguez was denying all responsibility, which wasn't a surprise. The guilty hardly ever admitted their crimes, but if he was involved, Ethan suspected he wasn't acting alone. He didn't seem driven enough and definitely lacked in the brains department. If they could link the Tetrodotoxin to him, then maybe they could find out who was pulling the strings. Emily had her contacts scouring their records for evidence of restricted toxins being procured or obtained via less-than-legal means, but the research was going to take some time. That meant their best bet was to locate the accomplice. Right now, he was leaning toward the agent. If Rodriguez wouldn't talk, then maybe Roth would. After all, he'd spent his whole career speaking in a loud voice about his many clients, making sure the whole world knew who they were and what they represented. Now was his chance to do the right thing and say something worthwhile.

His phone rang, jerking him from his thoughts. He answered it.

"Steele, we have a problem." It was the Chief.

"I have a lot of problems right now, Chief. Not least, trying to get these people to talk."

"Well, then brace yourself because you have two more particularly gnarly curveballs coming your way."

Ethan shook his head. He needed more problems like he needed a letter from the Canada Revenue Agency. "Go on."

"I took a call from the airline. Looks like we have a whole 737s worth of reporters, photographers, and general lowlife scumbags touching down in Churchill as we speak. Word has it, they're heading your way, and fast."

"Great. That means they'll be camped outside our door along with Harper Mayfield and her crew. I guess there's no way of stopping them?"

"No, not really. That's out of my remit to control, except…"

"Except what?"

"Well, that kind of leads me to my second point."

"Which is?"

The chief exhaled. "There's a bad weather front coming your way, Ethan. A real ass-kicker of a storm. The weather reports say you could be seeing three feet of snow overnight, maybe more. Strong winds, too."

Ethan glared out the window. The snowfall was already starting to worsen. He suspected they could be snowed in by the morning if it got any worse.

"That's just what we need," he said, drumming his fingers on the table. "As if this job wasn't hard enough."

"Well, yes and no. Those reporters won't be able to make their way out to you for an hour or two, which means..."

"Maybe the snow will block the roads before they can get here."

"Ethan, my boy, you hit the nail on the head."

As the call ended, Ethan wondered if anything was going to break their way. He'd never worked a case where everything was so intertwined and twisted into so many loops and knots. On the surface, Elena Hart was the perfect professional, a person whom everybody loved and whom the press adored. However, in her death, they were uncovering strained relationships, affairs, obsessions, violence, and inner circle tensions that had been invisible to the outside observer. It all led to a complex game of cat and mouse, and right now, the mouse was winning.

Ethan eyed the board, which he and Emily had been keeping updated but hidden from the other residents as they learned more and more about their live-in suspects.

At the center was Elena Hart. Lines then snaked from the circle they'd drawn around her to each of the airplane's passengers: James Bateman, the conman of a boyfriend who was having an affair with Lily Craven, Elena's best friend and makeup artist. Cue a line to Lily from both Elena and James. Then they had Tom Oates, the disenfranchised photographer who hated the art of celebrity and resented Elena's lifestyle. Sarah Locke was next, with her admittedly volatile relationship with Elena, and then there was Samantha Mitchell and Leo Bryant, who had lines connecting them to Elena but also to each other after their affair had been revealed. The only other people left were Mike Rodriguez, the Air Marshal who had an unhealthy obsession with the person he was getting paid to protect, and Max Roth, the agent who they now suspected had ten million dollars to gain in the event of his client's death—a client who they now knew was planning on leaving him. Ethan stood and drew a red circle around both Rodriguez and Roth before connecting the pair of them with a thick red line.

He was starting to feel like the net was closing in, and little by little, they were cornering their prey into a side street they couldn't escape from. It wasn't just the snow that was cutting off the roads to the training lodge. The evidence was coming down like the storm from hell, and it was going to make every way out damn near impassable.

Chapter 8

The Calm Before

Max Roth was once more in the chair, but this time, his smug grin had been replaced by a look of steely defiance. Ethan doubted whether Sarah Locke had tipped him off about her big reveal, which meant the agent had to have figured out for himself why they'd called him back in.

"I thought we'd said all there was to say," Roth said, breaking the silence. "I mean, you know everything about me, and yet I know very little about you."

"Some information has come to light, Mr. Roth," Emily said. "Some things we think we need to know more about."

"As I said, I told you everything about the relationship Elena and I had. Whatever you think you found, it's not true."

"But how can you say that without knowing what it is?" Emily countered. "Don't you at least want to hear it?"

"Don't want to, don't need to. We have a saying in the profession, Dr. Carter. If what people are saying sounds and smells like crap, it's probably crap. I suspect what you're about to tell me fits into that category, and I don't want that stink on me."

Ethan watched the interchange between Emily and the agent. It was the way he and his partner had decided to play it. Emily would lead the early exchanges and he would watch, deciding which way he would direct the interview once the time was right. Since her training, Emily had become a skilled interviewer, having been trained by the same guy that had trained Ethan—his mentor, Charles Schaeffer.

"Tell us about your business, your revenues, and how much your profits relied on Elena Hart, Mr. Roth."

"I told you already. She was my A game."

"So, you relied on her a lot?"

"I'm in the process of diversifying," he shot back. "Representing reality stars, a few athletes, some company presidents. I'm not a dumbass, Doctor. I've known for a long time now that what I had with Elena couldn't last forever. Nothing ever does."

Ethan made a note of the agent's appearance. He was sweating.

"What would your business do in the event Ms. Hart ceased to be a client, Mr. Roth?" Emily asked, pushing the point home. "We've looked at your records, and it appears that over 70 percent of your earnings come directly from Ms. Hart's activities."

"Activities that I helped arrange," Roth added, his lip curling into a sneer. "Don't forget, I built her up, dragged her off her ass, and put her in front of some of the best modeling agencies in North America. Elena would still be strutting in cheap heels up and down the trash-covered streets of downtown Detroit if it wasn't for me."

"So, you believe that Ms. Hart's fame is a direct consequence of your efforts?"

"Damn straight."

"That must have bugged you," Emily said, skillfully manipulating the exchange, "that she was wealthier than you could ever dream, and yet, to paraphrase what you just said, everything she had was because of the opportunities you presented to her."

"I do just fine," he replied, his eyes narrowing. "I can't complain. I've lived a good lifestyle off the back of Elena's career. Could I use more money? Sure. Couldn't everybody? But that doesn't mean I resented her for it."

"But she was your 'A' game, Mr. Roth. She was over seventy percent of your income. If she walked away from you, she'd put you out of business."

Max Roth shifted in his chair, eyeing Ethan as he checked his watch. "Where are you going with this?"

"As I said. New information has come to light."

The agent stood and paced the room, running his hand through his hair, which was looking increasingly slick with sweat. "Look," he said, "If you're about to tell me what I think you are, then you're wasting your time. It has nothing to do with this case."

"But you already said there was nothing left to say," Emily replied. "You even cast doubt over what we had."

"Because it's not relevant. Because although I regret it, it really has nothing to do with Elena's death. I would never get myself involved in such a thing. I would never."

"Why don't you sit back down," Ethan interjected, gesturing toward the chair. "And tell us what it is you think we have."

The agent fiddled with his cuffs before wiping a handkerchief across his brow. He was looking decidedly uncomfortable. "I'm guessing you scoured my phone records and found some of the messages I sent to Elena. I knew I should have used a burner phone, but I was getting desperate."

"About what?" Ethan said, taking control of the interview, nodding to Emily, who leaned back in her chair.

"Stop playing games," Max said. "If you've called me back in here, you know enough already."

"True," Ethan replied, "But we need you to confirm it."

The agent sipped his water, glugging it as if it were his last drink before his execution. "I came across the information by accident. I hadn't been looking, I swear. I took a call from an ex-business associate of Elena's who was still pretty upset about what she did. I paid him off, of course, because Elena was still making her name at that point, and I couldn't have anything getting in our way, but the information he told me was pretty explosive."

Ethan was suddenly intrigued, realizing that what Roth was telling them had nothing to do with the celebrity insurance policy he took out in the months leading up to Elena's death.

"Tell us about this information," he said. "How explosive are we talking?"

Roth nodded. "As you know, Elena didn't have any money when she started out. She could barely afford to switch the lights on in her apartment. She was that broke. What this guy told me was that she had signed up to support a charity raising money for a local sports facility, and initially, she had used her growing public persona in the local area to bring in thousands of dollars, but as the pot of money began to grow, and Elena's own fortunes hit the rocks, she'd started to withdraw money from the account, a little at first, but then more and more until she'd taken over half the funds for herself."

Emily eyed Ethan over the frame of her glasses. This wasn't what they had expected at all.

"So, she stole the money. How much are we talking?"

"A little over ten grand," Max replied, "Which is ironic because, in the grand scheme of things, these days, that's not even a drop in the ocean. But back then, back when she could barely pay for her own lunch or keep a roof over her head, that kind of money meant a few months of being able to sleep without worrying about who was going to come knocking on her door."

"And the charity didn't notice this money missing?"

"Not at first, no, and by the time they'd realized what had happened, Elena had moved on and was flying all over the country, modeling for some of the biggest names in fashion."

"So why didn't they go to the press right then and there?" Emily asked. "Why wait?"

"Because, at this point, there was nothing to say," Max replied. "Once Emily had the money she owed, she slipped it back into the account. Nobody would have even known about it if it wasn't for the charity's accountant picking up an anomaly, and once he did, he decided to call me. All he wanted was some money to guarantee his silence, and that's what I gave him. Fifteen grand for the ten that Elena borrowed."

"So, what did you do with this new information?" Emily asked.

"I buried it for a few years. Kept it in my back pocket. There's another saying in this industry, Doctor. One bullet in the chamber is worth ten in the clip. I kept that bullet for a long time, suspecting that one day I might need it."

"But why?" Ethan asked. "What could you possibly gain from keeping information about your client's prior misdemeanor hidden from her?"

"You didn't know Elena, did you, Detective?" Max replied.

"No, I never had the pleasure of meeting her."

"Then you wouldn't know what kind of person she was. Her sense of morality was precious to her, as was her public persona. She believed that people in her position had to show the best to the world and that she had an obligation to prove to her fans that those in the public eye could set an example for people. You remember I told you about how we lost some jobs because of Elena's moral code? That's exactly what I'm talking about."

"So, if this news ever got out," Emily chimed in, "It would have destroyed that image."

"Exactly, Doctor. That's exactly what I mean."

"So, what happened next?" Ethan asked. "You said you kept this bullet in the chamber, but I'm pretty sure at some point you pulled the trigger."

Max turned his head away. "I got greedy," he said. "Saw all the money coming in and thought I deserved more than my fair share."

"So, you blackmailed her?"

He chewed his lower lip. "This was after I started to hear rumors that she was looking elsewhere, so I confronted her, telling her that if she signed up with another agency, I'd take it to the press. She was upset, of course. Elena had a temper on her—I'm sure Sarah Locke told you all about that—and she threatened to sue me if I dared tell anybody. But she knew there was nothing she could do. I had the ammunition, and she was unarmed. She offered to pay me, and I took the bait, demanding a monthly bonus on top of my commission to guarantee my silence."

"How much money are we talking about?" Emily asked.

"In total, I'd say around a million bucks," he replied. "Maybe a little more. That kind of money meant nothing to Elena. She was bringing three times more than that home in a week. It was barely pocket change."

Ethan decided to throw in the little grenade he and Emily had been holding back. "Tell me about the celebrity insurance policy."

Max Roth's face darkened. "Who told you about that?"

"You know as well as I do that we can't reveal our sources."

"That policy was a matter between myself and my broker. Nobody should know about it."

"So, you're admitting it exists?"

The agent slammed his hands onto the table. "This is outrageous."

"I suggest you calm yourself down, Mr. Roth. We're just doing our jobs here."

"So, I assume you now think I killed Elena to cash in on the insurance policy?"

"Did you?"

"No, I did not!"

Emily stepped in. "Look at it from our perspective, Mr. Roth. You've just admitted to blackmailing Ms. Hart, something we were unaware of until you volunteered the information, and now you've confirmed you took out a policy on Ms. Hart's life just months before she was killed."

"Oh, I see!" the agent hollered, standing up once more. "So now the great detectives have decided that those things add up to a guilty verdict. Well, I can tell you right here, right now, Detective Steele and Dr. Carter, I had nothing to do with Elena Hart's death. I loved that woman like a sister. Yes, I made mistakes in our relationship, and yes, I got greedy, but I would never have hurt a single hair on her head. You have to believe that."

"So why the policy?" Ethan asked. "Why did you insure your client for ten million dollars?"

"Because she was a high profile celebrity, Detective, with a lot of admirers, some of whom were verging on sociopathic. I read her fan mail and looked at her social media posts. These people were crazy. We did everything we could to protect Elena, including hiring security for her flights, but I was also a realist. The chances of someone getting through were growing with every new photoshoot and every high-profile appearance. I took the policy out to protect all of us. I'm sure you've noticed, but there are a lot of people out there who relied on Elena for their livelihoods, and when this policy pays out, it will go some way in helping us all to stay afloat."

The agent was shaking now, his face twitching. Tears lingered in the corners of his eyes. Ethan had the guy down as an accomplice in Elena Hart's murder, but now he wasn't so sure. With everything they had on him, a lesser man might have folded, but Max Roth looked like he'd lost someone close to him as if he really believed that he and his client were like family.

"If you have anything else to tell us," Ethan said. "Anything else you've been keeping from us, then now's the time to reveal it. No more secrets, Mr. Roth. We need to know everything."

Max slumped onto the chair with his head in his hands. He looked completely spent.

"Then I suggest you talk to the stylist and the freelance photographer," he said. "Because from what I hear, they weren't Elena's biggest fans."

***

"So, what do you think?" Ethan asked after the agent had left the room.

"He seemed genuine," Emily replied.

"You don't think he was faking it?"

"No, it was too real. Those emotions just flowed from him, as if he really misses Elena. That doesn't mean he didn't kill her, though."

"Do you think he did?"

Emily shook her head. "I don't know. The guy's got motive times two, but I just didn't get the feeling that he was the murdering kind."

"Maybe he got Rodriguez to do it for him."

"Maybe, but those two don't seem close enough."

"Close enough to commit murder?"

Emily nodded. "I mean, they would have to have some kind of relationship to make it work, right? Like that case we worked over in Vancouver. The girl and her cousin who murdered their grandparents. Those two were almost symbiotic."

Ethan remembered that one. The grandparents had been buried in the yard, just beneath the barbecue where the murdering grandchildren stood cooking hot dogs.

There was a scream from outside, and Ethan leapt up, running to the window. The snow was falling really hard now. Everything was a sea of billowing white.

"What is it?" Emily asked, racing to his side.

"Is somebody out there?"

"I don't know. Maybe."

He ran out of the office and headed to the door just as it burst inward, filling the room with an icy gust of freezing air and swirling snow. A woman slumped to the floor, her body covered in blood and ice.

"Sarah," Emily said. "What the hell happened?"

Outside, there was growling noise, and Ethan looked up to see a creature emerging through the veil of snow—dark eyes, heavy snout and bloodied teeth.

"Quick," Ethan cried. "Help me get Sarah inside."

Max and James were the first on the scene, taking the unconscious woman's arms and dragging her across the floor, leaving a crimson smear of blood behind her.

The polar bear seemed intent on finishing the job it had started, but Ethan had no intention of letting it inside.

"Come on," he said to the others. "It's coming."

Sarah's feet were still blocking the doorway, and Ethan could see the bear was closing on them, only ten feet away, nine feet, eight feet.

"We have to get this door closed."

Emily grabbed Sarah's bloodied legs and swiveled her body, managing to move her just far enough inside before the polar bear raced onto the porch, coming within three feet of the doorway before Ethan slammed it shut, dead-bolting it as the bear crashed into its metal exterior.

"Jesus," Max said. "What the hell was she doing out there?"

"Smoking, I guess," James replied. "If anyone needs a reason to quit, there it is, right there."

Emily turned Sarah onto her back to inspect her injuries. Her jacket was ripped open across her abdomen, and there was a gash in her stomach. Her left leg was also badly wounded, with a long laceration from the top of her thigh to her knee. While no internal organs appeared to have been impacted, she was losing a lot of blood.

"We need to get her a hospital," Emily said. "And we need to apply pressure to these wounds."

Lily ran into the store cupboard and came back with a pile of towels. Emily took them from her, bent down, and tied one around Sarah's leg tightly, making a makeshift tourniquet and cutting off the flow of blood to the leg wound.

"What about her stomach?" Samantha asked.

"It needs suturing," she said, "cleansing, too. But for now, we need to apply pressure."

"Can't you do that? Aren't you a doctor?"

"I'm not a surgeon; I'm a pathologist and detective, and in any case, I don't have the supplies needed for injuries of this severity. It would be impossible for anyone to repair the damage that's been done in these conditions."

Max was already on the phone, yelling at the emergency services. "They say they can't get to us," he said, his hand over the receiver. "Apparently, the snow's too deep, and helicopters can't fly in this weather."

"But they have to," Samantha replied, her voice quivering. "If she doesn't get to a hospital soon, she's going to die."

Sarah opened her eyes as the realization of her predicament dawned on her. "Bear," she said, peering down at the blood pouring from her wounds. "Didn't see it. Came out of nowhere." She cried out in agony.

"Try to stay calm," Emily said, trying to sound convincing. "We're going to get you the help you need."

Ethan peered out the window. They had a truck, but he knew it would be no good in such deep snow. They'd make it maybe a quarter mile before they'd get stuck, and with the polar bear out there, it wasn't worth the risk. He didn't know what to do. Sarah was literally bleeding out on the rug, and yet they had no way of getting her to a hospital.

Emily peered up at him. She was gripping the young project manager's hand so tightly that her knuckles were white. "How do we get her to the hospital?"

He couldn't let Sarah die like this. He couldn't let this woman lose her life because of his investigation.

There was a loud crack outside and the sky turned a fluorescent red. Ethan went to the window, just as the air became filled with the sound of approaching engines. He saw the crimson flare overhead as it slowly fell to the ground and the polar bear galloping away over deep snow drifts.

"What the heck is that?" Leo asked, opening the door.

"What are you doing?" Emily said.

"Don't worry, the bear's gone. Look."

Ethan stood in the doorway and watched as two headlights approached, the first stopping just short of their vehicle and the other nearing the front porch.

"Who is it?" Emily asked.

"I have no idea," Ethan replied.

He grabbed his coat, pulling it tightly around him as he stepped out onto the porch. He felt the sharp bite of the blizzard.

"Detective Steele," a woman said, stepping off the snowmobile. "I think my friend and I can help you?"

"I'm sorry," Ethan said, trying to figure out why he recognized this woman's voice. "Do I know you?"

"You do. We've met many times." She reached up and removed her goggles, revealing the beaming face of the reporter who'd already caused him so much trouble.

"Harper Mayfield," he hissed.

She grinned. "The very same. Look, I saw what happened between Elena's project manager and that bear, and I figured you needed some way to get her to the hospital."

"We really do. She's in a bad way."

"It's not going to be comfortable for her, but if I strap her onto the passenger seat of my photographer's snow sled, I think we can get her there."

Ethan never thought he'd be so happy to meet a journalist. "You'll need to hurry. She's lost a lot of blood already. My partner tied a tourniquet around her leg, but the wound in her abdomen is bad."

James and Max helped him lift Sarah from the floor. Thankfully, she'd already slipped out of consciousness. The three of them replaced her coat before carrying her to the vehicle, and they used straps to tie her to the snow sled.

"You're a lifesaver, Harper," Ethan said. "Literally."

"Well, I never thought you and I would be working on the same team, Detective," she replied. "Maybe we should do this more often."

"You stick to your lane, Harper. I'll stick to mine. Right now, I need you to get Ms. Locke to the hospital and fast."

"I'll do my best."

"And, Harper, this stays out of the press."

"If you agree to give me an exclusive interview after you find out who killed Elena Hart."

Ethan chewed his lower lip. She had him right where she wanted him, and he hated it.

"Do we have a deal?" she asked.

"Let's talk about that later. Right now, Sarah needs to get to the hospital."

The reporter smirked as she adjusted her goggles. "By the way," she said, swinging her leg over the snow sled. "Don't rush to blame the bear. Polar bears rarely attack humans unless they feel threatened, startled, or mistake someone for prey. If Sarah was out here alone in the dark, smoking a cigarette..." She paused for emphasis, her expression thoughtful. "The sudden flare of her lighter might have caught the bear's attention, confusing or alarming it. These animals are curious by nature and driven by survival, especially in these harsh conditions." "We know these are unusual circumstances for all of us," Detective Steele said.

She gunned the engine and the two snow sleds sped off into the distance, leaving Ethan standing on the ice, praying that they made it in time.

He climbed the steps to the porch, stepping over the smear of crimson beneath his feet and the bloodied handprint on the stoop. He headed back inside, closing the door behind him. Emily sat on the floor, Sarah's blood on her chest and neck. Lily stood behind her, her face ashen.

"Is she going to be okay?" she asked.

"We just have to hope they make it across the snow," he replied.

He helped Emily to her feet, and they shared a knowing glance. They'd flown out here to help solve a case, and now one of their key witnesses could die. Was this how his career was going to end? With blood on his hands?

He looked at each of them: at Samantha Mitchell, who looked like she'd seen a ghost; at Tom Oates, who appeared increasingly agitated; at James Bateman, who was trying with limited success to clean the blood from his fingers; at Max Roth, who was now one of their chief suspects; at Leo Bryant, who seemed more concerned about his photography gear than the badly wounded project manager; and at Lily Craven, who was shivering as if the cold had gotten to her.

"Wait," he said, running the names of the passengers through his head. "Is there someone missing?"

Emily scanned the living area. "Yes. You're right. Where's Air Marshal Rodriguez?"

"I thought he was out there with you," Samantha said. "It certainly looked like he was planning to help get Sarah onto the snow sled."

"I didn't see him out there," James replied.

"Me neither," Max added. "And it's not like you could miss him. The guy's a monster."

"He has to be out back," Emily said, heading toward the storage area. "Mr. Rodriguez? Mike? Are you there?" She disappeared through the door before re-emerging, shaking her head.

"I guess the guy didn't like the food," Leo said.

Emily glared out the window. "He can't have gone out there. He'll die in the blizzard,"

"I'm going after him," Ethan said, zipping his coat.

"Are you kidding me?"

"We can't let him get away."

Emily opened the office door. "Detective, can I speak with you privately for a moment?"

"But we're losing time."

"Please!"

Ethan followed her into the office as the others looked on.

"Look," she said, closing the door. "It's admirable that you want to find the Air Marshal, but you saw what happened to Sarah. And you can also see what it's like out there. I mean, I'm guessing you can see the wind and the snow. You'll be dead before you make it two miles."

"That's okay," Ethan said.

"Okay? How's that okay?"

"Because Rodriguez will know that, too. If he's smart, he'll be in one of the outbuildings, hiding among the training equipment and box files."

"You don't know that."

"Emily, he's ex-military. He's no fool. He'll know this storm is bad, so he won't take any chances."

"But he took a chance by making a run for it. Look, I think he's dangerous, and I think you're taking an unnecessary risk."

Ethan knew she was right, but what choice did he have? He'd almost lost one of the civilians in his care. He wasn't about to lose another.

"Look, Em. He's one of our prime suspects, and even though we've not been able to link him to the Tetrodotoxin yet, you and I both believe he had something to do with Elena Hart's murder. If he's running, that's just proved to me that he knows a lot more than he's telling us, and I'm not about to let that go."

"So, you're willing to risk your life?"

"Isn't that what we do, Em, every time we take a case like this? You and I have both looked into the eyes of the Grim Reaper more than once and lived to tell the tale. This is no different."

He opened the door and went to leave, but he turned back, seeing the fear in her eyes. Perhaps they'd worked too many cases together. Maybe they were closer than they should be. Relationships affected objectivity; that's what his mentor had told him. "Never let your emotions get in the way of facts and evidence, Ethan," Charles Schaeffer had said to him over a beer. "If you find yourself getting too close, step away, maintain the distance. Your responsibility is to the case, not to those around you." He'd tried to follow that mantra ever since Rebecca had been killed, but Emily and him, they'd become a solid team, two individuals who together made a better whole. He valued that.

"Look," he said. "I'll take a radio. Anything happens, I'll give you my location and you can come find me."

"You'd better believe I'll be there," she said, turning her head away. "Just don't do anything stupid."

He didn't answer, knowing whatever he said would only make things worse. He eyed the others as he opened the door.

"The rest of you, stay inside," he said. "Dr. Carter will take over the interviewing process while I'm away. In the meantime, nobody steps outside of this building without her approval."

As he walked out into the snow, he realized he was taking a big gamble. Sure, he was a trained detective, but the Air Marshal was an ex-soldier in the US Army. If he was going to find the guy, he would have to be smart. Emily was right; Rodriguez could be dangerous, and in a blizzard like this, the soldier had the upper hand.

Ethan spied the footprints in the distance just in time. He headed out, feeling the comfort of his shoulder-holstered pistol against his chest and hoping he'd made the right call.

***

Emily stood in the office, wondering what her next play was. Rodriguez was out there, running from the police, which painted him in a bad light, but that didn't prove his guilt. It was still possible that someone in the lodge was responsible for Elena Hart's murder, and Ethan had already suggested there could be more than one individual involved in her death. She had to keep working on the angles and consider every possibility.

They'd narrowed their suspects down to the Air Marshal, the boyfriend, and the agent, but the way Bateman and Roth jumped to Sarah Locke's rescue made her doubt their prior assumptions. Maybe they'd missed something. Maybe they were letting the crass personality traits of the conman and the sleazeball cloud their judgement.

She ran everything back through her mind. Max had pointed her in the direction of Samantha and Leo, claiming they had something against Elena, but when she'd spoken to them, it had turned out the whole thing was a dispute over small sums of money, nothing major, and the pair seemed more interested in each other than anything that was going on around them.

That left two people: Elena's best friend, Lily Craven, who'd been remarkably quiet ever since her affair with James Bateman had been revealed, and Tom Oates, who was an enigma.

She logged into the office computer and looked up the photographer's record. He'd been busted when he was in his twenties for possession of weed, but only a baggy. Other than that, he had two unpaid parking violations dating back to 2008. It was hardly a red flag. She tried a Google search of his name and found what they already knew—he'd landed a big contract in Hollywood to carry out several shoots on the Paramount lot, but his friend and business partner, Terence Harding, had got them kicked off the program over some dealings he'd had with the studio's booking agent. Tom had gone off the radar for a few years after that before resurfacing as Elena Hart's personal photographer and documentarian.

All of this she knew. None of it was a surprise. She leaned back in her chair and exhaled. Ethan was out there pursuing one of their suspects through a snowstorm, and all she could do was sit in the office and carry out meaningless Google searches. She felt so useless.

Then she thought of something. The story about Tom Oates losing the Paramount contract had almost entirely focused on Terence Harding being the loose cannon, but what if Tom had known what was going on? What if he wasn't the innocent party the press had made him out to be?

She looked up the guy who Tom's business partner had apparently bribed, and found he was a booking agent named Hank Rothchild, an agent who was involved in the movies, but also had an interest in fashion. Rothchild was one of Paramount's top guys, but he didn't work directly for them. He had his own business, which had grown astronomically since he'd started out on the streets of Detroit.

That piqued her interest, and she dug a little deeper. The Detroit business had focused on catwalk models and high-end fashion shows. Rothchild had initially been the sole booking agent for Michigan Fashion Week, which, back when he started, wasn't that big a deal. However, she thought the link to Detroit, Michigan, Elena Hart's hometown, was worth pursuing. She kept searching, and sure enough, when Emily did a deeper search, using an AI tool to match faces with photographs, she pulled up an image of the bald-headed Hank Rothchild standing alongside none other than the glamorous supermodel.

She didn't know what that meant, but she suspected the pair's association was more than just a coincidence. Elena had been booked by the same guy who had allegedly taken a bribe to get Tom Oates the Paramount contract. She did the same search again, this time adding Tom's picture into the AI tool, and after the browser spent some time running through its records, it eventually spat out a second photograph, this one of Elena, Hank, and Tom sitting side by side at a Louis Vuitton show in Chicago.

She shook her head. This was too much. Maybe the murderer had been staring them in the face all along, and they'd been too distracted to see it.

She hit print before approaching the window, wondering what Ethan was doing now and whether he was safe. She glared at the radio, remembering how he had told her he would call it in if he got into any trouble. He'd only been gone fifteen minutes, but if he was still out there after thirty, she'd radio him and find out what was going on.

She opened the door and headed toward the print room, and that was when she saw Tom Oates standing there with the printed image in his hand. He looked down at it, the realization dawning on his face.

"Mister Oates—Tom—that's mine. I printed that. I didn't mean for you to see it until I'd had time to—"

Before she could react, Tom grabbed a knife from the kitchen counter and wrapped his free arm around Lily's throat.

"Don't come any closer," he said, backing away toward the doorway that led to the outside lab. "You make a move, and Elena's little bitch friend here dies."

"This is crazy," Emily replied. "I was just going to ask you some questions about your dealings with Hank Rothchild, nothing more."

"Yeah, I've seen how that goes down," he hissed. "Sarah almost got herself killed after you interviewed her, and now the detective's out there pursuing Rodriguez through a blizzard. No thanks. Not me. I've got a right to defend myself."

"You have, but not like this."

"I'll do it any way I please," he said, pushing the door open. "You come after me, Doctor, and there'll be even more blood on your hands. Much more."

Chapter 9

Frozen Lies

The weather outside became increasingly treacherous as Ethan pushed through the snow and ice, following the footsteps left by the Air Marshal. He pulled his goggles over his eyes and his hat down over his ears, and tried to protect his exposed skin from the freezing temperatures. Whatever Rodriguez had been up to, it had been serious enough for him to venture out across the tundra, risking his life in what were life threatening conditions, not to mention the roaming polar bears, one of which had seriously wounded Sarah Locke.

"Rodriguez," he yelled, trying to make himself heard above the burgeoning winds. "Rodriguez! Give it up. You can't get away. Just come back inside, and we can talk this out."

There was no answer, which didn't surprise him. People rarely came out with their hands up, like in the movies. Rodriguez was a soldier, which meant he was prepared to fight.

Ethan stepped through the blizzard, crossing the car park, which was now beneath a thick blanket of white. He spied the media tent that Harper and her photographers had set up at the perimeter of the property. It was barely withstanding the constant onslaught from the ferocious winds and swirling snow, but Ethan knew it was a possible hiding place.

He drew his weapon—a Glock 17—and approached with caution, carefully placing one foot in front of the other with the gun held out front.

"Rodriguez, if you're in there, I'm coming in. Don't do anything stupid. I just want to talk."

He pulled back the hanging white canvas of the thick tent and peered inside. A battery lamp burned on the far side, while in the middle of the tent there were tables covered in leftover food containers, drinks bottles, and cigarette cartons. Harper had obviously sent the rest of the crew home when the storm had begun to build, leaving her and her lead photographer alone and able to rush Sarah to the hospital. He only hoped they made it in time.

The tent was consumed by long shadows, stretching from floor to ceiling, moving and flickering as the covering canvas flapped and rippled. Ethan stepped over the threshold, keeping to the darkness as he slipped along the perimeter, watching for any signs of movement. Rodriguez knew about fighting in close quarters, and Ethan knew that quarters didn't come much closer than this. If the Air Marshal wanted to, he could be on Ethan in an instant. He had to keep his wits about him.

"Rodriguez," he said again. "If you're here, be sensible and come out and talk. You're not under arrest. We just want you back inside where it's safe."

There was a noise outside, and something brushed the side of the tent. Ethan's eyes darted to his right, watching for signs of movement in the entranceway. There was another noise, followed by a shaking of the tent wall, causing Ethan to step hastily backward. He stood that way for a moment, second-guessing what was going on, before rushing to the doorway and stepping outside, only to be confronted by a polar bear pawing at the tent covering. Ethan's breath caught in his throat as he backed away. The bear had its back to him and hadn't noticed him yet, but that didn't ease his terror. He slowly slid to the side, putting the tent frame between him and the hungry animal.

The bear clawed at the ground, sniffed the tent, and then approached the entrance hatch. Ethan knew that roaming polar bears in Churchill rarely attacked humans unless they were confronted, so he stepped very deliberately and carefully, making sure he didn't make any sudden movements.

The thing was enormous, easily three times the size of him, with long claws, sharp teeth, and powerful arms. He didn't want to upset it at all, so he walked away, never turning back as he heard the bear tossing things aside inside the tent, no doubt devouring the half-eaten sandwiches and Cheetos.

Breathing a sigh of relief, he knew It had been a close call, but not the confrontation he'd been expecting. He eyed the collection of outbuildings on the other side of the compound and knew that Rodriguez was in one of those. He had to be.

If he was going to locate the suspect, it had to be now.

***

Harper rode her snow sled behind her photographer, Darren's, vehicle, the unconscious Sarah Locke strapped to the rear seat. The terrain was almost impossible to pass. The snow drifts had grown to over eight feet tall in some places, taller in others, and the snow was coming down so hard that visibility was extremely limited.

She'd seen the polar bear attack as it unfolded, which was hardly surprising. She'd been watching the lodge almost constantly since they'd got there shortly after the detective, the doctor and Elena Hart's entourage had shown up. She knew Churchill was renowned for its high number of polar bears, and although they weren't particularly aggressive to the human population, she also knew sudden, misplaced actions could startle them, and sometimes that was all it took. Bear safety is a big deal in Churchill for all who live there and visit; there is a safety video in the airport terminal for everyone to watch; if they are paying attention, they will know what to do or, in this case, not do.

Of course, the others wouldn't have known that particularly not the young project manager who had come outside a couple of times to smoke in the past few hours. She looked particularly stressed as if the whole experience was starting to grind her into the ground. She wanted to go over there and tell her to be careful, to warn her that using her lighter and being out by herself at night could very well cause the bears to react, but Harper was so obsessed with getting the next big story that she didn't want to alert the woman to their presence. Who knew what Sarah Locke was hiding? Some small part of her thought that if she just sat there and watched, Sarah might reveal something with her actions, or somebody else might step out onto the porch with her, perhaps revealing an association that could be important to the story.

The only thing she saw was a frightened young woman who just wanted to be anywhere but there. When she'd slipped the Marlborough

Red between her lips, she hadn't seen the bear walking among the vehicles, and when she'd flicked the lighter, touching it to the end of the cigarette and inhaling, blowing out smoke as if she were exhaling all her anxiety and fear, she never saw the polar bear move toward her. The poor girl never stood a chance.

Harper knew she could have stopped the attack from happening if she had warned her, but she'd been frozen to the spot. The guilt burned like acid in her gut as she watched the young woman get brutally savaged. Because of that, there was no way she could leave her there, bleeding out on the floor like a dog. She had to do something.

She needed to get Sarah Locke to the hospital, and she needed to make sure she lived. No other outcome was acceptable.

***

Emily turned to the others, who were all looking to her to tell them what to do. Out of all the possible scenarios that could have played out, the one she least expected was Tom Oates taking Lily Craven hostage in the makeshift medical examination facility.

"I'm going after them," she said. "But you all need to stay here. You understand that? You do not follow me, no matter what happens."

"But what if he kills Lily?" James said, his voice trembling. "What if he does something unthinkable to her?"

"He won't."

"But what if he does?"

"Look, it's my job to make sure that doesn't happen. You have to trust me."

"The guy was always a nutjob," Max said. "If it was down to me, we would have fired him years ago. But, Elena? Well, you know? She always liked the sad cases, the down and outs, and there aren't many out there more down and out than that guy."

Emily thought of the information she'd found on Tom, his association with Hank Rothchild, and the agent's association with Elena. The photograph she'd retrieved from the internet was obviously too much for the photographer to bear, and sensing the net was closing in, he'd reacted. She didn't know what that meant yet, but she did know that Lily Craven wasn't going to die because of it.

"Just stay here," she repeated and grabbed her jacket before stepping out onto the partially covered walkway. The snow had piled up all around the narrow passage, and she had to step sideways to make her way through it. Outside, the wind was kicking up a storm all around her. She hoped Ethan was okay. Sarah, too.

The doorway to the lab stood before her. She stopped outside, not knowing what to expect or even where Tom had taken Lily. If they were still inside the lab, that meant they were there with Elena's body. It was a grim thought: a suspected murderer standing beside his victim with a knife at another woman's throat.

She reached for her weapon—a Walther P99—and opened the door.

The lab was dark, bathed only in the green glow of the expensive equipment. She could see the curtained-off area where Elena lay and the trays of instruments lining the walls. She stepped inside, using the rear wall as her guide, keeping her back to it as her weapon wavered in her hands. The whole room was silent except for the persistent hum of the generator. There was nowhere to hide in here, nowhere to hunker down. If Tom and Lily were inside, there was only one place they could be.

"Tom," she said. "Tom, let's talk about this. Why don't you let Lily go? You can come back inside with me to discuss the photograph. Nobody's accusing you of anything here. We're just investigating."

"If you think I believe that, you're even more stupid than your partner," he replied, inadvertently alerting her to his location.

"No, Tom. Look, I'm telling the truth. It's our job to investigate every possible lead, but that doesn't mean everything we look into will lead us to the murderer. I'm sure you have a perfectly reasonable explanation for your association with Hank Rothchild. I'd just like to understand it, that's all."

"You come any further inside, Doctor, and you'll be investigating another dead body."

"Dr. Carter!" Lily screamed. "This guy's a lunatic! You have to help me!"

The curtain around Elena Hart's body shook as there appeared to be a struggle inside. Emily moved swiftly, striding across the floor at pace before grabbing the curtain and pulling it back. There, standing beside the semi-covered corpse of Elena Hart, was Tom Oates. The knife was across the throat of a terrified Lily Craven.

"I told you not to come any closer," the photographer hissed. "Do you want more blood on your hands? Do you?"

Emily had the gun trained at the photographer's head, but she knew she couldn't take the shot. It was too risky.

"Just drop the knife, Tom. It isn't worth going out like this?"

"Isn't it? You think this life's still worth living, do you?"

"I think you're better than this."

"You don't know me."

"Nobody deserves this, Tom. Not you, not Lily, and especially not Elena. I mean, just look at her. She had so much to offer the world, so much still to give, and now she's lying here in a cold room, no longer able to fulfill any of her dreams."

Tom scoffed. "You didn't know Elena, not like I did."

"Don't you dare bad mouth her," Lily said. "She was my friend."

"A friend? Really? Is that what you do to your friends, Craven? Screw around with their boyfriends while their backs are turned?"

Lily grimaced. "It wasn't like that."

"It sure looked like that from where I was standing. You think we didn't know what was going on? The rest of us? You'd have to be blind not to know that you and Bateman were fucking. The only person that didn't know was the one person that mattered. The one person who should have been told. And now she's dead."

The photographer's voice cracked as he said those last words as if the supermodel's untimely demise was almost too much for him to take.

"I really want you to drop that knife, Tom. It would make this exchange a lot easier for Lily and I."

"I'm sure it would," Tom said, pulling Lily closer. "But I'm not about to give up my advantage. I let her go, and you shoot me dead, and all of a sudden, I'm a news headline. *Disenchanted photographer kills famous model*. You'll get your murderer, the press will get their story, and I'll just become a statistic. No thanks. I think I'd rather stay right here."

"Look," Emily said, releasing the clip from her gun as she lowered it. "See. I'm not interested in hurting you, Tom. I just want you to let Lily go."

The photographer seemed to think about it. "I didn't kill her," he said. "Even though you think I did. It wasn't me. I would never have hurt her."

"So why the photograph with the guy you claimed you didn't know? Why blame the loss of the studio deal on your partner when you'd been in bed with Hank Rothchild all along?"

Tom's shoulders seemed to sag. "Hank was a creep, a real sleazeball, but he had contacts in the right places, and it turned out he knew this young, up-and-coming model in Detroit. I was doing a bit of paparazzi work back then—not my finest work, I'll give you that—but Hank liked to use me to boost his clients' profiles. This was before that leech, Max Roth, ever got involved. That was the worst hire Elena ever made, let me tell you that, but that's another story.

"Anyway, Elena and I hit it off right away. She had a great sense of humor back then, and believe it or not, when I was younger, I was quite the joker. She liked to laugh, and I liked to make her laugh. We were a good team. Hank would tell me where she was going to be, and I would encourage all my paparazzi friends to come with me to snap her coming out of a restaurant or movie, that kind of thing. I'd sell the photographs to buddies of mine in the press; Hank would pay them to run a story, throw in some dirt, like a local model seen with a movie star or pretty woman having dinner with a *committee member*, something like that, and little by little, Elena's stock began to rise."

Emily shook her head. "But why the whole story with the Paramount deal? And why did you deny ever knowing Rothchild?"

"As I said, Hank was a sleazeball, a grade 'A' slice of crap. Elena needed him to get her career off the ground, which is why she put up with him, but the guy had wandering hands."

"You mean he touched her?"

"Are you kidding? He couldn't keep his hands off her. Whenever she walked by, he'd slap her ass, or he'd accidentally walk in on her while she was getting changed. Elena would tell me about it, and I'd threaten to find the guy and kick the crap out of him, but she'd never let me. She just wanted to be famous, you know? She'd have done anything for it, even put up with a lowlife like him."

"She never mentioned any of this to me," Lily scoffed. "I'm her best friend. I would have known."

"You think she went around telling people that she let her agent get handsy with her? No way. I knew, but I wasn't going to tell anyone."

"But you're telling me," Emily replied.

"Doesn't seem to matter now," Tom said, staring at Elena's motionless body.

"So what's the connection here, Tom," Emily said. "What am I not getting?"

The photographer sighed. "I liked a drink back then. I guess I still do a little, but not like then. I could sink a bottle of bourbon in one afternoon and still be ready for work the next day. The problem was, it made my anger come out, and one night, after I'd had a heavy drinking session in the city, I decided to confront Hank. He was in another bar with a buddy of mine, so I confronted him, told him I didn't want him touching Elena anymore. He took it badly, denied everything, but I could see it in his eyes. He was enjoying me coming after him. He got off on stuff like that. He was sick in the head. Something snapped in me, and I hit him, knocked him flat on his ass. He started cursing and swearing at me, so I hit him again and once more for luck. I left him there, bleeding out of his broken nose and split lip."

"What did Elena say when she found out?"

"She never did. I never told her, and neither did Hank. I guess he was too ashamed. He never touched her again, though. He wouldn't dare. A month later, he left town, and suddenly, Max Roth was on the scene. That was when I got out. To this day, I'm still not sure who's worse."

"And then your company got the Paramount contract."

"Right. Or, at least, my partner did. This was three years later. I knew Hank was the agent, but he didn't know I was in on the deal. I told Terence to keep me out of it, thinking that once the contract was signed, it wouldn't matter. I didn't know money had changed hands or that Terence had done some under-the-table deal. When the studio found out what had gone down, they canceled the contract, but Hank still walked away with fifty thousand dollars of our money. I think he'd found out I was part of the team and leaked the deal to the studio execs just to get back at me. That bastard cost me over a million dollars."

Emily let out a long breath. His story sounded believable, and if that were true, it meant he wasn't their guy. He looked like a beaten man, as if life had kicked all the fight out of him.

While both Emily and Tom were distracted, Lily took her opportunity and threw an elbow into her kidnapper's ribs, knocking the air out of him as she punched him in the face. Tom fell to the floor, the knife skittering across the tiles.

"You expect us to believe that?" she screamed. "That you didn't kill Elena? You're the only one in this lodge threatening anyone with a knife, Tom! You ever think about that?"

"I loved her!" he yelled, his voice hoarse and cracked. "I didn't kill her because I was in love with her. That was why I beat the crap out of Rothchild. Because he was hurting her, and I couldn't stand to see the woman I loved being put through that kind of abuse."

"Oh, give me a break."

"I'm sorry, Tom," Emily said, cuffing him. "For what it's worth, I believe you, but I can't have you kidnapping innocent people."

Emily took no pleasure in arresting the guy or reading him his rights, but he'd left her no choice. The only problem was that his story blew yet another lead out of the water, meaning they were left with one guy and one guy only—and he was hiding out in the snow with her partner on his tail.

Chapter 10

Storm of Suspicions

Ethan was starting to shiver. The cold was getting to him. He wasn't used to these temperatures or the sheer force of the blizzard. He needed to get inside as quickly as possible, but he knew one false move could prove deadly. He was pursuing a trained killer. He had to keep that thought in his head.

The three outhouses surrounded a small central area where the training officers parked their vehicles. With no other vehicles around, Ethan's location was totally exposed. If the Air Marshal had armed himself somehow, then he was a sitting duck. The safer option was to move into one of the buildings and use the shadows as cover.

He tried the door to the building closest to him, but it was locked. However, one of the windows was open, so he pulled it with his left hand, keeping his back to the wall and his gun trained on the darkness. He half expected the window to explode outward in a hail of gunfire, so he stood there for a moment, watching and listening.

Satisfied that nobody was planning on blowing his brains out, he climbed inside, rolling over a wide table and dropping to the floor. He sat there for a minute or two, letting his body acclimate to the warmer temperature. He was so cold he could barely move. The only time he had ever felt anything remotely similar was during a training session in Chicago when he and his team had been asked to pursue an actor pretending to be a criminal along the shore of Lake Michigan in the middle of winter. At the end of that exercise, Ethan had felt like a walking corpse.

Once he'd gained some feeling back in his fingertips and limbs, he removed his goggles and studied his surroundings. The room was a typical storage area, filled with racking, box files, and assorted computer equipment.

He moved up the first aisle, peering through the shelving, looking for any signs that somebody had been inside. He stepped over a computer monitor and a nest of tangled wires, using his feet to clear the way while attempting to remain as quiet as possible.

Eventually, he made it to the end of the aisle and rounded the shelving unit. The next aisle was much darker, and both sides were piled high with boxed files, which blocked out any light from outside.

He started forward, controlling his breathing while moving his feet as carefully as possible. He could barely see anything at all, meaning he had to use his hands to trace the lines of the shelves on either side of him to ensure he moved in a straight line. The darkness was like an amorphous blob ahead of him, an insidious, undefined thing that, nevertheless, filled him with dread. He didn't like not knowing what lay in wait. He was the kind of person who had to be in control, had to know what was coming.

He stepped forward, but his foot slipped on something, almost sending him tumbling.

"What the heck?" he whispered, dropping to the ground and touching the floor. It was damp. He raised his fingers to his nose and sniffed. There was no odor. He touched it once more and realized the liquid was cold. It dawned on him at once. He'd stepped in melting snow, which could only mean one thing. Rodriguez had been through here.

He leapt up and moved swiftly, pacing along the aisle, now more certain than ever that he was in the right place. He didn't see the file that had been left between the aisles or the cables that had been pulled tight across the walkway. When he hit the makeshift trip wire, he went staggering forward, grabbing the shelves for balance and inadvertently pulling them down on top of himself. There was a loud clatter as boxes and metal shelving slammed into the ground and buried him beneath a pile of paperwork and stationery.

"Damn it!" he hissed, trying to regather his composure, while to his left, a shadow suddenly moved, jumping over one of the desks and heading for the window.

"Rodriguez!" he yelled. "What the hell are you doing?"

The Air Marshal leaped up onto the sill, looked back into the shadows, and then jumped through the window and out into the snow.

Ethan threw the shelves and paperwork off him, staggering to his feet as he ran along the aisle, around the desk, and toward the door. He flicked the deadbolt and opened it, just in time to see Rodriguez disappear into the furthest building. Before he slipped inside, Ethan saw something that filled him with dread. The Air Marshal was carrying something he recognized. He'd somehow found a handgun, which meant this situation had just escalated dramatically. It was no longer a game of hide and seek with a potential suspect. It was now a deadly pursuit, one in which the stakes couldn't be higher.

***

The road ahead was blocked by a tree that had fallen in the storm, which meant Harper and her photographer had to steer their snow sleds into the forest to navigate around it. The situation was now becoming almost impossible, and what's more, they were running out of time. The hospital was still over half a mile away, and at the speed they were going, they were bound to be too late. They had to go faster. Suddenly, something came to her.

"Head toward the railroad!" she hollered, screaming above the winds.

"What?"

"I said we need to go toward the railroad!"

"It'll take us longer to go that way!" Darren replied. "You sure you want to do that? I think we can get through here if we keep going."

"No. It'll be clearer. I'm sure of it. If we can make it to the tracks, we should have a straight shot to the hospital!"

Darren nodded his understanding before leading them through a small cluster of trees and out onto the tundra. Their vehicles raced up a steep mound of snow before leaving the ground, sending ice and debris flying as they hit the other side and sped into the distance.

Harper's hands were numb and her face frozen, but she was determined they would get the wounded woman there in time. They had to.

"There!" she called out, pointing into the distance. There was a faint rise in the snowdrifts, signaling a long, straight-raised area of land. It stretched to their left toward the town. Harper's plan was to ride the snow-covered railroad track right into the heart of Churchill as if they were taking the train. The tracks ran along the western shore, past the Bear Cafe and the Churchill Hotel. There, they would leave the track and head northeast toward the Churchill Health Center. She only hoped they made it there in time. This couldn't all be in vain. It just couldn't.

The railroad was now less than a quarter mile away, so close she could almost touch it, and they pushed harder, driving the snow sleds close to their top speed, but then Darren's sled seemed to hit something beneath the blanket of white, and it skidded out of control before tipping on its side, sending Darren and his unconscious passenger tumbling into the snowdrift.

"No!" Harper cried, dismounting her sled and running toward them. "Sarah! Darren!"

Sarah Locke was lying on her back, blood oozing from her wounds, but apparently with no further injuries. Darren, on the other hand, sat upright with a cut cheek and his right arm bent at an acute angle.

"Is it broken?" she asked.

Darren grimaced. "I think so. Hurts like a bitch."

Harper felt like screaming. They were so close. How could fate be so cruel to them?

"Take her," Darren replied. "I can hide out beneath the bus shelter until you come back."

"You'll freeze," Harper said. "You'll never survive out here."

"I'm from Montreal, Harps. They build us tough in Quebec. Anyway, once you make it there, you can send someone to come get me."

Harper stood there, not knowing what to do. Darren was her go-to guy, her pal, her sounding board. They'd been working jobs together for almost ten years, and he'd never let her down. Not once.

"I don't know."

"I do. Now, just do it!"

"You sure you'll be okay?"

"I'll be fine," he said through the pain. "Just get her to the hospital before it's too late."

***

Emily stood in the lodge, eyeing Tom Oates, who was handcuffed to a pipe. She couldn't take any chances with him, even though she knew he wasn't their killer. Lily still hadn't forgiven the guy. The makeup artist glared at him with malicious intentions. He'd held a knife to her throat after all, and while Emily believed he never truly meant to do her any harm, it was still assault with intent, and that carried a sentence.

"Where's the detective?" James asked. "And where's Rodriguez? It's obvious he was the one who killed Elena. The innocent don't flee from the scene of a crime."

Well, actually, this isn't the scene of the crime, so really your theory sucks, Emily thought to herself, but decided not to be so petulant. "I'm sure Detective Steele has this all under control," she said. "We just need to give him some time." But she wasn't sure she believed that. The storm was getting worse than ever, and the terrain was becoming even more impassable. If Ethan didn't get back soon, he might not get back at all.

She could see Lily and James weren't speaking, which added additional tension to the room. Everything was unraveling all around them—the lies they were telling her and Ethan, but also the lies they were telling each other. Lily hadn't known James any more than Elena had, and none of them had known what secrets their wealthy boss had been keeping.

She glared at the radio. Ethan had said he would signal her if he ran into trouble, but what if trouble had already found him, and he had no way of calling? What if he was lying out there now, bleeding and freezing to death, while she sat in here with a cast of rogues, any one of whom could have been involved in Elena Hart's death?

"Maybe I need to go find him," she said.

"What, and leave us in here with the crazy photographer?" Max cried. "You have to be kidding me? This guy is unhinged."

"I might be unhinged, but at least I don't con my clients out of everything they have," Oates spat in reply before turning to Bateman. "Or screw my boss's best friend."

"Hey!" James yelled. "What the hell did I do to you?"

"Let's all just calm down," Leo chimed in. "I mean, what do we have to gain from arguing?"

"Easy for you to say," Tom said. "You're one of the only guys in here who hasn't seriously been considered a suspect."

"That's because I've done nothing wrong. Unlike you, Tom, I don't go around threatening innocent women."

Tom pointed to Elena's stylist. "No, but you don't mind using her any time you feel like it."

"What did you say?" Samantha cried. "I don't know what you've heard, Tom, but Leo and I aren't an item."

"You are when he wants you to be."

Samantha turned to the freelance photographer. "Leo? What have you been saying to him?"

Leo held up his hands. "Whatever he's heard, he hasn't heard it from me."

"Okay, okay!" Emily cried. "You're all acting like a bunch of spoiled kids. I need you to be grownups for me, okay? We have a detective out there who is risking his life to save one of your colleagues, and all you can do is bicker among yourselves. Miss Craven?" she eyed Lily. "As Elena Hart's oldest friend and the only one around here who seems to have any common sense, can I count on you to keep an eye on things while I go check on Detective Steele?"

"Sure. I guess. I mean, I'm not sure these people will do as I say, but—"

"Good," Emily said, pulling on her coat. "Because we're all trapped in here together. You're going to be roomies for as long as this storm lasts, and the whole experience will go a lot smoother if you can at least try to get along."

She opened the door and stepped out onto the porch, knowing things were about as bad as they could get, and the only way to make them better was to catch Rodriguez. If anybody knew what happened to Elena Hart, it was him.

***

Ethan pushed through the snow as he headed toward the larger, two-story building. The door that Rodriguez had entered stood ajar, the snow making its way inside through the narrow crack.

He was now even colder than ever, his body becoming a rigid slab of ice as he pressed himself against the wall, checking that his gun hadn't jammed in the sub-zero temperatures. He wasn't even sure if he could hold his arm steady enough to aim properly. If he waited outside any longer, he probably wouldn't even be able to move his legs. This had been a bad idea, to begin with, and now it seemed like the worst plan imaginable. Trailing a trained soldier through blizzard conditions was the equivalent of skydiving without a parachute, and now this trained soldier was armed with what looked like a Smith and Wesson 3953, stolen straight out of the training center's armory.

He peered through the crack, waiting to see if anybody would come at him. This time, Rodriguez had turned on the lights. The outbuilding was an administration building lined with offices and cubicles. In here, it was going to be even harder to find the Air Marshal hidden among the many partitions and filing cabinets. The only good thing was the relative warmth. Rodriguez must have had the good sense to switch the heating on.

He stepped into the hallway and pulled the door closed behind him, sealing the heat in and the freezing temperatures out. He didn't stand around long enough to enjoy the soothing sensation of the warm air blowing on his cold face. He couldn't get too comfortable. Rodriguez was lying in wait for him somewhere in this building. For all he knew, he had his sites trained on him right now, waiting for him to make a move before he squeezed the trigger.

"I know you're in here!" he hollered, trying to reason with the suspect. "Let's just talk this out."

There was a sound from up ahead, and Ethan poked his head around the corner just in time to see Rodriguez darting across the corridor.

"Come on, Mike," Ethan said. "This is crazy. It's freezing outside. Why don't we head back to the lodge and talk about this like grown men?"

There was no answer, just the gentle hum of the air conditioning. Ethan knew he had a choice to make. He could either stand there and try to negotiate with a guy who was clearly unwilling to talk, or he could take matters into his own hands. The second option had a higher degree of danger, but it was currently the only option worth considering.

He took two deep breaths, braced himself, and then darted across the hallway, running diagonally into a cubicle. Just as he slid inside, the partition behind him splintered as a bullet blasted through it and ricocheted off a metal cabinet, shattering a computer monitor. He held his hand over his head, trying to protect himself from the glass and timber splinters.

"What the hell are you doing?" he hollered. "This doesn't have to be like this."

He peered around the corner of the partition as he tried to calculate the likely location of the Air Marshal. The angle of the bullet had been shallow, meaning he was probably located in the conference room at the end of the hallway. The distance from the cubicle to the conference room was around 50 feet, which was way too far for him to make a run for it unnoticed. The only way he was going to get there was to keep making the diagonal sprints from room to room, a dangerous maneuver that increased his chances of taking a bullet.

It now seemed more likely than ever that Rodriguez was their guy. Innocent people didn't open fire on a police officer. Ethan hadn't anticipated it going down like this. Everything had been under control until the PM had been attacked by the polar bear. Since then, everything has gone to hell. He shook his head. It was always the things that you didn't expect that bit you in the ass. He'd been chasing lead after lead, interviewing witness after witness, when all the time, the Air Marshal had been right in front of them, selling them a line that they'd somehow bought. The evidence had all pointed to him, but Ethan had allowed himself to be distracted by press releases and side plots, all of which amounted to nothing. This was what it all came down to a standoff between him and a guy that had charmed his way into Elena Hart's life with the sole intention of killing her.

"Lay down your gun, Mike. It's not worth it. You kill me, you'll be looking at a double homicide charge. Come out with your hands up now, confess what you did, and maybe they'll look a little more kindly on you."

There was another loud crack, and the window to the right of Ethan's position shattered. Ethan took the opportunity to move and ran across the corridor into the office, which was two rows up. A bullet hit the ground as he dove inside, and another smashed into the open door. Whatever his intentions, the Air Marshal was serious.

Ethan checked his own weapon. He had a full clip: seventeen rounds. He'd been hoping he wouldn't have to use his gun, but that outcome was looking more and more unlikely. His heart was pounding in his chest. No matter how hard he had trained or how many cases he'd worked, nothing had prepared him for coming face to face with an armed aggressor. Nothing came close to the fear of taking a bullet, of potentially losing your life, but that was the job. Find the bad guy, neutralize them, and bring them in. He had a duty to Elena Hart to bring her murderer to justice, and if that meant putting himself in the line of fire, then that was what he was going to do.

He chanced another peek along the hallway, took a second to compose himself, and then made another dash toward the office kitchen. Just as he leaped through the open door, there was another loud crack, and his leg exploded with intense, fiery heat, followed by a sticky wetness. He looked down to see the blood on his pants and the entry and exit wound through his calf. He bit down on his lip, trying to stifle the scream. The pain was almost unbearable. His vision swam in and out of focus as he felt the nausea kick in. He lay back against the wall, waiting for the agony to subside, hoping it would. He'd been hit, which meant he was now less mobile than he needed to be. He suspected Rodriguez had aimed for his leg for that exact reason. Slow him down. Prevent him from making another move. Buy himself time.

Ethan ripped the leg of his pants and looked at he wound. It was a clean exit, which was good. No lasting damage, but he suspected he'd be limping for the foreseeable future. That was if he made it out of this alive.

There was the sound of footsteps from the direction of the conference room. That was very bad. Maybe Rodriguez was coming to finish the job. Ethan kicked back toward the far wall, putting as much distance between himself and the open door as possible. If the Air Marshal was planning to kill him, he was going to make it as difficult for him as possible. He reached up, grabbed the counter, and pulled himself upright, trying to ignore the agony in his lower leg as gravity pushed more blood toward the gaping wound.

The footsteps were close now, no more than ten feet away. Ethan raised his gun and pointed it toward the doorway. He thought of Rebecca, of the first time they'd met, their first kiss, the moment he had proposed to her, and the magical feeling when she'd said yes. He'd never been so happy, so excited about the future they would build together. Their wedding, their home, and perhaps children one day. That had all been taken away from him when that bastard had killed her, snuffing her life out just like that, like a flick of a switch or the shutting off of a faucet. Maybe that was what death was like. A simple shutting down. He wasn't planning on dying today. That wasn't how this was going to go down. He had a job to do, and damn it, he was going to do it.

He held his finger to the trigger and steadied his hand as Air Marshal Mike Rodriguez stepped out into the open, his own gun raised.

"I thought I clipped you," Rodriguez said, eyeing the wound. "Don't worry, I wasn't aiming to kill."

"Then why do you have your gun trained at my head right now?" Ethan replied.

"I could ask the same question of you."

"You shot first."

"You forced me into it."

There was something in the Air Marshal's eyes. A darkness, a resignation. He looked like a man who had nothing left to lose, and in Ethan's experience, those were the people you feared the most.

"I told you it didn't have to go down this way," he said. "I told you to lay down your gun. I only wanted to talk."

"I'm done talking. We've been talking for days, but no matter what I say, you still think I killed Elena."

"Mike, you're the only guy who ran away and the only one who shot a police officer. This doesn't look good for you."

Rodriguez nodded, but his eyes never left Ethan.

"Yeah. I get that. But, you see, I have to defend myself. I can't just be a victim. I'm not that guy. When things get tough, when people come at me, I fight back, just like you did when your fiancée was murdered."

"And look how that panned out."

"Won't stop me fighting."

"But what are you fighting? What's it all for?"

"Life," Rodriguez said. "Pain. Hurt. You name it, I've experienced it. A dad who left before I was born, a crack addict mother, a foster care system that was more interested in dollars than the kids they were there to protect. Even the military had it in for me. I'm a nobody with nothing, a statistic in a database. Just a number."

"But you have to realize this isn't going to make things any better. Running out like that. Stealing a gun. Shooting me. Give this thing a positive end, Mike. Do the right thing. Hand me your gun, come back to the lodge with me, and give me your side of what happened."

The Air Marshal stood there motionless, his face impassive. Ethan thought the guy looked completely spent, as if every ounce of strength had evaporated.

"Elena was one hell of a beautiful human being," he said eventually. "Beautiful inside and out, like a clear-cut diamond. I'd never met anybody like her before. The way she looked, the way she walked, and even the way she spoke to people. She had a natural grace, you know? Like an angel. I could have just stood there and watched her for hours. You know the perfume she wears? I bought it. Sprayed it all around my room just so I could imagine being with her. Not in a creepy, stalker kind of way. Just so I could imagine what it was like to exist in her sphere, in her orbit."

He paused, seemingly thinking about his next words. Ethan let the silence hang in the air, not wanting to interrupt his flow. This was important. He knew that what the Air Marshal said next could nail the case.

"My mom had that perfume. Not the same. She couldn't afford anything like that. It was similar, though. The same sweetness to it. I used to sit there and watch my mom spraying it on as if she thought it could hide the smell of weed on her or the vodka. My mom had an addictive personality. Whatever she took to, she became addicted to it. Caffeine, cigarettes, even men. The guys she brought home were all assholes, every single one of them. She loved the bad boys, the guys that would treat her nice for a few days, maybe a week, and then they would beat up on her, sometimes me too. I was too little to do anything about it then. I used to hide in the closet and watch it happen, too afraid to breathe.

"You know, when she was young, my mom was beautiful. She looked a lot like Elena. Same color hair, same height and build. Same grace. She could have been a movie star, too, if she'd put her mind to it, but she met a guy, and that guy got her into some bad stuff. As I said, my mom had an addictive personality. Once she was hooked, she was hooked bad. Way I see it, those men that did that to my mom, they were the same as the person who killed Elena, only they did it in a much smarter way. You get arrested for shooting somebody—you don't get arrested for driving somebody to addiction. Seems wrong to me."

Ethan watched as Rodriguez's shoulders sagged. He was reliving a trauma that had shaped his life and, perhaps, had caused him to do the unthinkable. It was a story Ethan knew well. He'd seen it in so many cases. The traumatized kid who grows up and eventually repeats history by doing the exact same thing to those around him. It was a cycle that was difficult to break.

"You love your mom," Ethan said. "I can see that. But that doesn't excuse what happened to Elena, does it?"

The Air Marshal shook his head. "No, it doesn't. Not at all. She didn't deserve what happened to her, the same way my mom didn't deserve it. They both had so much to offer to the world."

"And now she's back there in the med lab," Ethan interjected. "Because somebody poisoned her."

"Like my mom was poisoned," Rodriguez replied. "Like I said. Those people who killed my mom were never convicted because, in the eyes of the law, they did nothing wrong. Where's the justice in that?"

"There isn't any," Ethan said. "But two wrongs don't make a right. Killing someone through lethal injection because that's what happened to your mom is still a crime, Mike. Just like shooting a police officer is a crime. The only way this ends well for you is if you hand in your gun to me and surrender."

Rodriguez's eyes narrowed. "See!" he yelled. "This is exactly what I'm talking about. You've had me pegged for this all along, no matter what I said. You think, just because I had a few posters on my wall of Elena, and because I may or may not have been able to get my hands on some of the toxin you say killed her, that I was the guy who did it."

"Then come back with me and prove you're innocent."

"There's no point," Rodriguez said, thrusting his handgun forward. "Don't matter what I do or say. I'm your prime suspect, and you and your partner need to crack this case. You'd convict me faster than the bullet that went through your leg. People like me don't get a fair crack at the law, Detective. We get whatever fits the narrative, and in this case, the loser ex-soldier profile matches your lazy idea of a murderer right down to the way I was raised and the way I act. Well, I'm not going down for Elena Hart's murder, and if I have to kill you to make sure I don't get my ass hauled into the nearest jail, then that's exactly what I'm going to do."

He raised the handgun, aiming it directly at Ethan's head. The detective knew he had two options. Talk fast and hope he could convince the guy this was a bad idea, or take the shot and potentially kill an innocent man. Either way, he had a millisecond to think, which was no time at all. He touched the trigger, knowing if he was going to shoot, he had to do it fast. Rodriguez was on the verge of firing his own weapon. He could feel his pulse racing, the sweat on his brow, his whole life culminating in this one critical choice. Everything moved in slow motion as Rebecca appeared in his subconscious, telling him what to do. If it was going to be him or the Air Marshal, there was really no choice to make at all.

"Drop the gun, Rodriguez!"

The Air Marshal's eyes switched to his right just as Ethan went to pull the trigger.

"I said drop your gun!"

It was Emily. She was standing there with her own gun raised, her feet placed shoulder width apart. Ethan didn't know how, but she'd made it into the building unnoticed.

Rodriguez shook his head. "I'm not going to prison."

"You are if you don't hand me your gun," she replied. "Be sensible. Do the right thing. I don't want to shoot you."

Rodriguez eyed the Walther in her hands and sneered. "You're going to arrest me anyway."

"True," she said, glancing at Ethan's wound. "You've shot a police officer, which means we have no choice, but unless we can prove you killed Elena Hart, that's where this stops."

Something shifted in him as if all the fight had disappeared. He lowered the gun. "I just wanted to protect myself."

Emily moved quickly, grabbing the Smith and Wesson and cuffing him. Rodriguez slumped against the wall.

"You sure you're just the medical examiner?" Ethan said, limping toward his partner.

"I couldn't let you have all the fun, now could I?"

As they led the suspect back to the lodge, Ethan used his partner's shoulder for support, and he knew they had their work cut out. Something about the Air Marshal told him he wasn't their guy, which meant somebody else was. It was like a never-ending puzzle with an impossible solution, but they had to find it. Somebody on that plane killed Elena Hart.

Chapter 11

Frostbitten Truths

"Quickly," Harper hollered, watching as the nurses pushed the gurney containing the motionless body of Sarah Locke. "She's badly injured and has lost a lot of blood."

"We'll do everything we can, Ms. Mayfield," the doctor said.

"You'd better because I work for a very influential publication, and if something happens to her, it will be all over the morning's news."

She slumped into a chair and took a breath. She felt bad for threatening the medical staff, but the woman needed urgent attention. She looked like she only had minutes left. Her face was so pale, her body limp. Her chances of survival were slim at best.

Harper ran her hand through her thick curls. She was exhausted, freezing cold, and emotionally spent. She'd ridden hard through the snow, desperately trying to get to the health center in time. Darren's crash by the railroad had lost them a lot of time, a time they didn't have. There had been so much blood, too much, as if Sarah's body was being literally drained.

She'd pushed the snow sled as hard as she'd dared, almost losing it when she'd left the tracks, but she knew she couldn't slow down. Every second was vital, not just for Sarah but for Darren. He was out there, hunkering down in a bus shelter while the blizzard intensified.

Harper knew this was on her. She could have done something before this all went down, but she'd put her own journalistic ambitions before the safety of others. Before everything. That was why her husband had left her and why she now spent every night working until she literally fell asleep at the computer screen, trying to blot out all the mistakes she'd made. And there had been a lot. The time she'd fictionalized a story just to make a headline stick. The supervisor she'd slept with on her way to making senior reporter. The co-workers she'd stabbed in the back for the sake of her career. At this point in her life, she was alone with no family, very few friends, and a social life that was barely breathing. The last thing she needed were the deaths of a young woman and the only photographer she'd ever formed any sort of relationship with on her conscience. Maybe it was time for a change. Maybe it was time for a new Harper Mayfield.

She thought of Elena Hart and the case she'd been following. Something about it wasn't right. The two suspects the police were following—the Air Marshal and the agent—didn't seem plausible to her. Neither had a real beef with the supermodel, and neither had any history of violence. Something didn't add up.

There was somebody else, however. Somebody she'd had her suspicions about all along and somebody she thought could have done it. They had the motive, the means, and the opportunity. Just maybe.

She pushed the thought aside. She had to focus. Darren was out there, and he needed help. She ran to the desk and told them to hurry. If her friend remained outside much longer, they were going to find a block of ice with a highly paid photographer inside.

***

Back at the lodge, the other passengers were growing restless. James Bateman paced the room, chewing his fingernails furiously, while Max Roth tossed a ball against a wall repeatedly, annoying Samantha Mitchel, who was fidgeting anxiously in her seat. Beside her, the freelance photographer, Leo, scrolled through his telephone, trying to find out when the storm was going to abate. Elena's lead photographer, Tom Oates, lay against the wall, his handcuffed to a pipe, looking like he could kill any one of them.

Lily watched each of them, knowing she'd been put in charge but wanting to be anywhere else. The tension in the room was unbearable. At any moment, a spark could ignite, and there was no way she could control the inevitable blaze.

The Air Marshal's dash for it had completely caught her off guard. He'd seemed so sure of himself, so calm. Sure, he had baggage, but who didn't? Every single person in that room had a reason to want Elena Hart out of the picture. The supermodel had been her best friend, but sometimes she could be a hard person to like.

"I've had enough of this," James said. "I'm getting out of here."

"You heard the doctor. She told us to stay put," Lily hissed. "And where do you plan on going, anyway? You won't even make a mile in that storm before you freeze to death."

"I don't care. Anything's better than waiting here for the cops to arrest one of us."

"Why would you say that?" Max interjected. "Have you got something to hide?"

"No more than you, Roth."

"I'm an open book, Bateman. Just do as Lily asks and sit yourself down."

"No, I think he's right," Leo said, becoming increasingly animated. "We're already two down, and that means the odds of one of us being thrown to the lions have increased significantly. Steele and Carter won't let us leave here until they have their murderer."

"They already have him, Leo," Samantha replied. "The guy who's made a run for it. That's why she's left us in here on our own. They catch the Air Marshal. They catch their bad guy. After that, we can all go home. The best thing we can do right now is sit tight."

Lily watched as the room fell silent, secretly wondering where all this was headed. Deep down, a little part of her wished Elena was there. They would laugh about what was going on in their usual secretive way, giggle about the infighting and backstabbing. The treachery had always been a part of the circus that was Elena Hart's life, but it had never been so blatant. These people weren't friends. They were associates, thrown together by circumstance, each of them with their own agendas and sideshows. Elena had known that. It was partly the reason she kept them all close. She enjoyed the tension, knowing that if the members of the team were focused on their dislike for each other, she would be kept out of the line of fire. Unfortunately for her, that strategy was only ever going to work for so long. Eventually, the pistol would be trained on her.

James's real identity had been a surprise to Lily, but it didn't really change things. She'd been slowly falling out of love with him anyway.

His deception just expedited the inevitable. The one thing it proved was nobody could be trusted, herself included.

"The Air Marshal didn't do it," Tom Oates said from out of nowhere.

"So now the kidnapper has an opinion," James snapped back.

"Hey, I made a mistake. I panicked. Doesn't mean I haven't been watching."

"You wanna tell us who you think did it, then?" Max asked. "What's your big theory? The butler with the candlestick?"

"I have my opinions, and I have proof, too," he said. "But the only person I'm telling is the detective."

"Which means you have no idea."

"Think what you like, Max. I don't care. Elena was the one I cared about, and now she's dead."

"Sounds like the kind of thing a murderer would say," James said, sneering.

"Why don't we all just keep our opinions to ourselves," Lily interjected, wondering what evidence the photographer thought he had. "Pretty soon, this will all be over, and each of us can go our separate ways for good."

And I, for one, can't wait, she thought. She'd had enough of the lot of them to last her a lifetime.

***

They made it back to the lodge, stepping under the cover of the front porch as the snowfall worsened. Ethan's leg was hurting more than ever, and his whole foot was soaked in blood. He pushed the pain away, sensing that their investigation was nearing a conclusion, even though they still didn't have any solid leads.

"Well, look who's come back to the fold," James said as they walked inside. "What happened, Rodriguez? You fall over on the ice?"

"Everybody stay where you are," Ethan said. "The doctor and I are going to put the Air Marshal in one of the holding cells."

"Cells?" Lily said before spotting the trail of crimson emanating from Ethan's shoe and the bloodied hole in his leg. "Holy shit. You've been shot?"

"I'm aware of that, Ms. Craven," Ethan replied. "As I said, everybody, stay where you are. Be assured that Dr. Carter and I have the situation under control."

"See. What did I tell you?" James scowled, approaching Lily. "This is even more reason for us to leave. The guy shot a police officer, and they want us to stay in the same building. They have to be kidding."

"Detective, I need to talk to you," Tom said.

"I'm a little busy here," Ethan replied. "And why are you cuffed to a pipe?"

"It's a long story," Emily said. "I'll fill you in when we have a moment."

"It really is quite urgent," Tom insisted.

"As I said, you need to give us a minute. At the very least, I need to find out what the hell's been happening since I've been gone."

They led Rodriguez to the rear of the building, where there was a holding cell for training purposes. Ethan opened the door and guided the Air Marshal inside while Emily followed behind with a makeshift tourniquet to slow the bleeding.

"So this is it," Rodriguez said, eyeing the tiny room. "All your promises of looking out for me and listening to what I have to say. That was all bullshit, right?"

"We still have a case to crack, Air Marshal. Right now, that has to be our priority."

"Don't you think I can help you? I'm a trained security guy, for Christ's sake."

"Maybe you're forgetting that you abandoned the lodge, stole a gun, and shot a police officer. Forgive me if I don't see you as a co-worker right now."

"But I saw things. I have information."

"And yet you've shared nothing useful so far."

"That's because you had me cooped up with the others where I couldn't talk freely. Even when we were in that interview room, everybody could hear what was being said. Those walls are paper thin, you know that, right? I'm out here on my own now. I can tell you things."

"We'll be back to talk to you later on," Ethan said, pulling the door closed and locking it.

"I mean it, Detective!" Rodriguez hollered. "I can really help you out here."

"You think he's telling the truth?" Emily asked as they walked away, Ethan leaning against her for support.

"I don't know what to think right now, but I do know we have to get control of those people out there. They look like they're on the verge of a walkout." He turned to her. "You wanna tell me what happened with the photographer?"

"Yeah. We had a situation while you were gone."

"Right. I could see that."

"The guy took Lily Craven hostage."

"Hostage? You've got to be kidding me. Why?"

"He said he thought we were trying to pin the murder on him."

"Why would he think that?"

Emily shrugged. "Maybe I kinda was. I don't know. I found out something interesting about the relationship he had with the agent who lost him his big contract. Did you know Tom Oates knew Elena Hart way back before she hit the big time?"

As Emily filled Ethan in on the photographer's run in with Hank Rothchild, Ethan stood there, his admiration for his partner's work growing with every passing moment. When he'd first started working cases with Dr. Emily Carter she'd been a dedicated medical examiner, a woman who knew everything there was to know about DNA testing and laser trajectory analysis, but little by little she'd become so much more.

"And now he wants to talk to us," Ethan said. "Do you find that suspicious?"

"Maybe he wants to talk himself out of the hole he's in."

"Or maybe, just maybe, something happened after you arrested him that triggered a memory."

"That doesn't make any sense."

"Nothing about this case makes any sense, Emily, and I'm done following the textbook investigation guidelines."

"Meaning?"

"Meaning we go back into that room, and we make those people talk."

"Not before you get that leg dressed," she replied, looking down at the bloodied mess the bullet had made of his calf.

"It can wait," he replied, limping toward the door. "Right now, we've got more important things to deal with."

"Ethan, if we don't sterilize the wound, it could get infected."

He whirled on her. "The only thing that needs sterilizing here are the lies we're being told, and I've had enough of dealing with them. Those people in there are going to tell us what happened on that plane, even if I have to drag it out of them."

***

Harper Mayfield sat in the waiting area, sipping a lukewarm coffee as she fielded message after message from her eager boss.

"Hey Harps," his message read. *"What's the latest?"*

Thirty minutes later, he added. *"It's been two hours since your last report. What are you doing up there? Playing blackjack?"*

And just five minutes ago, he texted her with, *"Harper, this story's going cold. I need you to breath some life into its corpse, and fast."*

She didn't know what to say to him. How could she explain that she'd witnessed a horrific polar bear attack and suddenly turned into Florence Nightingale? How could she tell her editor that she'd left her photographer in the snow and ice to save the life of a woman she didn't know? It was impossible to explain to somebody else when she couldn't even explain it to herself.

She tossed her cup and stood just as the front door opened. When she saw Darren being helped inside, his arm in a sling and his body wrapped in a thermal blanket like a freeze-dried meal, she ran to him.

"They found you!"

"Thanks to you," he said. "Without the tracker app on our phones, I could have been out there for days."

"It was a close call," the paramedic said, helping the photographer to a seat. "Another hour or two, you might not have been so lucky."

"Did she make it?" Darren asked. "Did she pull through?"

Harper shook her head. "I haven't heard anything since they took her in. Maybe I was too late. I don't know."

Just then, the doors at the end of the hallway swung open, and a doctor with neatly trimmed hair and a goatee strode toward them. "Harper Mayfield?" he asked.

"That's me. Do you have any news about Sarah Locke? Is she going to be okay?"

"You did a good thing getting her to us in this storm," he replied, removing his glasses. "She'd lost a lot of blood and was badly dehydrated, but we managed to patch her up and pump some fresh blood and saline into her."

"What does that mean? Is that good?"

The doctor smiled. "It means that with time and a lot of bed rest, she should make a full recovery."

"Yes!" Harper hollered, punching the air with both hands. "I mean, I'm so happy."

She turned to the photographer and hugged him, forcing him to cry out.

"Oh, sorry," she said, "I forgot about the arm."

She then went to the doctor and embraced him, too. For some reason, she was crying, which she hardly ever did.

"I'm sorry, Doc. I don't know what's come over me."

"It's not a problem," he replied. "You'd be surprised how often it happens."

He handed her a tissue before taking her to one side. "Look, this is a little irregular, but Ms. Locke asked to see you. I told her I thought it was too soon for visitors, but she was really quite insistent. I guess you two must be good friends."

"No, I've never met her before," Harper replied. "Not until I brought her here." The doctor's demeanor shifted, causing her to clarify. "No, it's nothing sinister," she insisted. "You see, I'm a reporter with the Chicago Tribune. Look, here's my business card." She handed over her details before gesturing toward her partner. "Darren and I were at the police training facility, covering a case Ms. Locke was involved in, when we saw the whole bear attack go down."

"Right," the doctor said. "Well, even if you don't know her, she seems to know who you are, and she wants to tell you something on the record."

"On the record?"

The doctor nodded. "She was quite specific about that."

Harper raised an eyebrow. "Well, I guess I have time."

***

Ethan and Emily arrived back in the living quarters to find James Bateman standing over the motionless body of Tom Oates.

"What the hell happened in here?" Emily yelled, running over to the photographer and placing two fingers on his neck.

"Don't look at me," Bateman replied. "I was just over there talking with Leo when the guy just slumped to the ground."

"Did anybody see what happened?" Ethan asked the group.

Lily shook her head. "One minute, he was telling us about a job he had planned; the next, he was on the floor."

"He's unconscious but breathing," Emily said. "Looks to me like he's been sedated."

"Sedated. But that's not even possible," Samantha replied.

Emily rummaged through the photographer's pockets and extracted a wallet, a phone, a set of keys, and a pack of gum. She raised it to her nose and inhaled. "Smells like mint," she said. "But I'd have to run some tests to be sure."

"Think, people," Ethan said. "Did anyone provide, or see anybody else provide, Mr. Oates something to calm him down."

Everybody in the group shook their heads.

"Come on. Somebody must have seen something."

"You gave him a glass of water, James," Lily replied. "I saw you do that."

James Bateman's head snapped toward her. "Are you implying something?"

"No, not at all," she said. "I'm just saying you were the last person to have any contact with Tom."

Emily removed the cuffs from the sleeping photographer, and together, she and Ethan carried him to one of the bedrooms, where they laid him down on his side to prevent him from choking.

"Where's the cup?" Emily asked the other.

"Over there, on the counter," James replied. "Look, the guy was thirsty, so I poured him a drink. He didn't want it at first, but after a little while, he seemed to change his mind, so I gave it to him. Never got a word of thanks, but that's Tom."

"So. anybody could have had access to the cup?" Ethan asked.

"I guess, yeah. I filled it from the faucet, then left it over there until Tom said he wanted it. Why? Do you think somebody dropped something in there?"

"It's possible," Ethan said. "Doctor, would you mind running some tests?"

"I don't exactly have everything I need," she replied, "but I think I could come up with a few possibilities."

She slipped on a pair of latex gloves, before grabbing the half empty cup and heading for the lab. Ethan watched her go before letting out a long breath. He'd never felt so out of control in his life. The group was reducing in numbers by the hour. At this rate, they would have nobody left to arrest by the time the sun came up.

"Okay," he said, grabbing his pen and notebook. "We've tried interviewing you individually, but that hasn't worked, so I recommend we do a little group activity. What do you say?"

"As in, we solve a puzzle together?" Max asked. "Because I'm really not into that kind of thing."

"Not a puzzle," Ethan replied. "A case. A murder investigation, to be precise."

The room fell silent as Ethan leaned back in his chair, rested his wounded leg on the coffee table, and looked at each member of the group one by one.

"Now," he said, forcing a smile. "Let's start at the beginning and see where the truth takes us."

***

Harper approached Sarah Locke's room and tapped on the door.

"Come in," Sarah replied, her voice slurred from the heavy sedation.

"The doctor said you wanted to see me," Harper said, gasping as she saw the young project manager's bandaged body and the bruising on her arms and chest.

"The bear got me pretty good," she said. "My own fault for smoking out there on my own. I'd even quit a few months back, too, but when the questioning got tough, the only thing I could think about was my cigarettes."

"Hey, don't be so hard on yourself. You were in a pressure cooker environment. Things can get kind of crazy when so many people are locked in together like that. You ought to see how cutthroat the newsroom can be."

They both laughed as Harper approached the bed. "How you holding up?"

"I've had better days, but the doctor told me it would have been a lot worse if it wasn't for you."

"My buddy out there did most of the work," Harper replied, knowing that was only half the truth. "I should have reacted sooner. If I had, maybe—"

"Hey, nobody's to blame here, not even the bear. It was just one of those things. Wrong place, wrong time," she eyed the pack of cigarettes. "Wrong habit, too."

"They say you'll make a full recovery."

"Apparently."

"I'm so happy about that."

"Me too."

"You want me to call anybody? Your husband? Boyfriend? Your mom?"

"No husband, no boyfriend," Sarah replied. "My mom's not a fan either. Truth is, Elena was my only real connection to the world, and now she's gone."

Harper took a seat by the bed. "What are you going to do now that's all over?"

"Find a new employer, I guess. Or change careers. This one is pretty stressful, and it takes up a whole bunch of my time, too. I guess that's why I'm single."

"Hey, you and me both. The curse of the working woman, right? Men can't stand the thought that the females in their lives might be more successful than them."

"Ain't that the truth."

"Maybe you and I should compare notes one day."

"If it comes with a large glass of wine, then you're on."

Sarah winced as she shifted on the bed.

"You okay?"

"Yeah. It just hurts when I laugh."

"Don't worry about it. Laughing's overrated."

Harper eyed the young woman. Her face was pale, and her eyes red-rimmed. She looked exhausted. "The doctor said you wanted to tell me something, but you know what? It can wait. I can see you're tired."

"No, I'm fine."

"Honestly, I'd feel better if you had a good night's sleep. I can come back tomorrow."

"In this storm? I don't think so."

"It's not so bad," Harper lied. "Look, I don't know what you want to tell me, Sarah, but you have to know, I'm a reporter for the Chicago Tribune."

"I know," the injured woman said, turning to face her. "And that's exactly why I wanted you."

"Because?"

"Because I remembered something when I came to, something that slipped my mind while I was being questioned by the detective, but now that I recall what happened, I can't get it out of my head."

Harper shook her head. "Look, while it's great that you want to tell me this new information, shouldn't you be talking to the police first."

"I'm not going back to the lodge, and unless I get this out now, I might lose whatever confidence these drugs are giving me."

Harper grabbed her notebook. "And you're happy for this to go on record."

"I'm more than happy." Sarah grinned. "Because once this gets out there, it'll blow the lid off the case."

***

Emily stood in the lab, waiting for the swabs she'd taken from the cup to come back with a reading. She watched as her breath fogged in front of her eyes, wondering what she'd done in a past life to get herself caught up in such a mess. What should have been a routine murder inquiry had turned into a game of cat and mouse where the mice were arming themselves and drugging one of their own. She didn't know what to make of it. She was even starting to believe Ethan's theory that there wasn't just one murderer among the supermodel's entourage. Maybe, she pondered, they were all in on it together, fighting among themselves for the right to Elena Hart's vacated throne. Perhaps that was the subtlety to the case that she and Ethan were missing. They were chasing down a lone wolf, but perhaps there was a whole pack baying for blood.

She thought about Rodriguez and how vulnerable he'd been. He'd suffered immeasurable traumas at the hands of his mother's many partners and had to watch her kill herself slowly through her own destructive addictions. Was it any wonder he had an obsessive personality, and that he craved the sort of attention he'd lacked as a child? Even though he'd attacked Ethan, she felt sorry for the guy. He was protecting himself the same way he'd had to protect himself when he was a young boy. She wasn't a psychologist, but she knew enough to realize that behavior like that was difficult to shift. It could be cured, though. Even a beaten dog can learn to get along with humans. Right now, the Air Marshal was emotionally broken, but that didn't necessarily make him a killer.

Ethan, on the other hand, was badly wounded and had refused even the most basic of treatments. That worried her. He was in there with the others, trying to unpick the tangled web of misinformation and confusion they'd been spun, and yet he'd lost blood, froze his ass off, and couldn't possibly be thinking straight. He could be frustratingly stubborn, which drove her crazy. He'd known it was a stupid move to go out in the snowstorm to chase the Air Marshal without backup, but he'd done it anyway. She couldn't figure out if the tragic loss of his fiancée had made him so self-destructive or whether he'd always been like that. Either way, if he kept walking so close to the flame, he was going to get himself burned. She couldn't let that happen. She cared for him, perhaps a little more than she should.

The analysis machine pinged, snapping her out of her thoughts.

She ran to the desk, fired up the laptop, and opened the report, scanning through the basic toxicology data before reaching the conclusion. What she saw made her gasp out loud.

***

"So, none of you guys saw anything out of the ordinary?" Ethan said. "Nothing at all, even though your boss was found dead mere hours after boarding the plane?"

"We've all been over this already," James said. "We were all in the other cabin. All except the guy who took Lily hostage and the other guy who shot you in the leg. It seems to be you're wasting your time out here talking to us when you should be in there talking to them."

"Tom Oates wanted to talk to me moments before he was rendered unconscious," Ethan said. "Do any of you have any idea what that was about?"

"As James said," Max replied, "the guy was a nutjob. If he was capable of kidnapping someone, he was more than capable of spinning a line to distract you."

"And yet it's entirely possible that somebody in this room drugged him while the doctor and I were putting the Air Marshal in a holding cell, meaning he never had the chance to speak with me. That seems pretty convenient to me."

"Are you suggesting somebody in here deliberately put him to sleep?" Samantha asked, eyeing Leo. "Because if you are, that means you truly believe the killer is in this room."

"Or you're clutching at straws," Leo said. "Which I think, given you clearly have no solid leads, makes perfect sense. Elena was a global media star, so I'm sure your boss is breathing down your neck to break this case. It's been way too long already, hasn't it? The people out there would have expected somebody to be in custody by now."

"I'm just stating the facts, Mr. Bryant. It's possible the killer panicked when Tom asked to speak to me and did something irrational."

"Or the guy drugged himself," Lily replied, standing by the coffee machine. "You didn't see him when he took me hostage, Detective. I'll never forget those eyes. The guy was clearly in a state of trauma."

"I don't want to speak ill of a fellow professional," Leo continued. "But Tom Oates is well known on the circuit for having a short fuse. The guy's punched more than his fair share of clients, let me tell you. That's why no one wants to work with him. No one except Elena, that is."

Ethan shook his head. "I don't buy it. Somebody here is telling a lie, and when I find out who it is—"

"With respect, that's your job, Detective, isn't it?" James interrupted. "To find out who's lying? To find out who killed Elena? It seems to me you're looking for us to dig you out of a hole when, in reality, it's you and the doctor who should be doing the digging."

Ethan sucked air through his teeth. Even though James Bateman could provoke his anger more than anybody else in the room, the conman had a point. He was in here swinging, trying to hit a home run on the last ball of the ninth with nothing but a rookie's chance. It was hopeless.

"Maybe you should just let us all go, Detective," Lily said, handing him a coffee while shooting him a sympathetic smile. "Come at this from a different angle when you've had time to think, and the weather outside isn't so damn horrible."

Ethan took the cup and placed it on the table beside him. "With respect, Ms. Craven, if I wanted a coffee, I would have asked for one, and if I wanted advice on how to be a detective, I'd call my boss."

Suddenly, his phone buzzed in his pocket, and he took a moment to bite down against his simmering anger before answering.

"This is Detective Steele."

"Detective, it's me, Harper Mayfield."

Ethan's frazzled mind fought to process the name. Eventually, he said, "How is she? Did you make it in time?"

"We did," Harper said, "and she's fine. A little beaten and bloodied, but she'll pull through."

"That's great news. Please tell her she's in our thoughts."

"I will, but I wasn't calling to give you a status update. I have something to tell you, something you're not going to believe."

He wondered where this conversation was headed. He'd been played by Harper Mayfield before, and it was never a pleasant experience.

"Is this legit?"

"As legit as anything I've ever reported on, Detective."

Ethan took a breath. "Then go on. What you got?"

"If you're with the others, I suggest you go into another room because the person who killed Elena Hart is not the person you think they are."

Chapter 12

Twisted Obsession

One Year Before – Tokyo, Japan

They sat in the dressing room of the Budokan, watching as dozens of stage hands rushed by and scores of models dressed in the latest designs out of Tokyo moved hurriedly toward the front of house. The PA system in the auditorium boomed with a pounding mixture of house and trance music as the host announced the next designer, while the crowd greeted the news with a rapturous round of applause.

Tom Oates moved around the room, snapping photograph after photograph, while James Bateman sat in the corner, watching TikTok videos on his cellphone. Samantha Mitchel rifled through the costumes, carefully laying out the first in a long line of dresses they were due to exhibit.

Max Roth came crashing into the room with his cell phone glued to his ear. "No!" he yelled. "That's not what Elena wants. She requested lobster ceviche, and what we have here is clam chowder. Can you see how that's different? Can you even contemplate how upsetting that is to her? You wanted the world's number one catwalk model at your show to boost your orders, and yet you can't even get a simple order right. We should walk right out of here now and leave you with egg on your face. How would you like that? What would something like that do to your precious reputation?"

Elena turned to see what all the fuss was about, interrupting Lily's attempts to apply her eyeliner.

"Just leave it, Max. I don't care about the damn ceviche."

Max raised a hand, signaling he was still locked in a verbal battle with the event's organizer. "Yeah, you'd better get it up here right away, you sonofabitch, or your show's gonna look like the world's most expensive cabaret without its headline act." He tossed the phone against the wall. "These people don't have a clue, you know that?"

"I told you to leave it. The last thing I need is another headline in the morning paper claiming I'm some sort of diva," Elena insisted.

"What am I always telling you, Elena? There's no such thing as bad press."

"Yes, yes, I know. You seem to be telling me that a lot recently."

The door opened again, and Sarah Locke walked in, a clipboard tucked beneath her arm. "The show's running behind, Elena," she said. "We might be here a little longer than we anticipated."

"How much longer?" James asked, setting down his cell phone.

"They're saying an hour, but I think it could be more like two?"

"Two hours?" James cried. "But we're supposed to be flying out of here tonight."

"Doesn't look like that's happening," Sarah replied. "Elena, what do you want to do? I can tell them the schedule's too tight and we're walking, or we can book a hotel downtown, and push the flight until tomorrow."

Elena turned to Lily. "What would you do in this situation?"

Lily shrugged. "I'd say one more night in Tokyo could be fun."

"Well, you heard her," Elena said, turning to the others. "I hope you packed your best clothes because tonight, we're heading out on the town."

Present Time – Churchill, Canada

Ethan sat in the office, the phone on the table, the last number he'd received a call from glaring at him from the screen. Harper Mayfield had so often been an enemy, a destructive force that seemed hellbent on putting leaks in every watertight case he'd ever pursued, but now she'd turned informer. What she'd said about Sarah Locke's time in Tokyo with Elena Hart was explosive stuff, and if it was true, it meant the killer was sitting in the living room, spinning a web of lies while everybody else sat there completely unaware. The killer had played a good game, allowing Ethan and Emily to pursue their wild theories while all the time, the real truth had been staring them in the face.

Well, not anymore. Now was the time to end this. He stood, intending to confront the killer head-on with this latest revelation, but suddenly, something slammed into his head, and he went staggering to the floor. He reached out and grabbed the table but missed it and sprawled onto his knees. Everything seemed to be made of Jell-O. He tried to turn to see who had hit him, but once again, something smashed into his skull, and in an instant, the lights went out.

"I don't think you'll be needing that," a voice said, reaching over and grabbing his cell phone and gun before heading toward the door. "You look tired, Detective. Why don't you stay in here for a while and sleep."

One Year Before – Tokyo, Japan

They sat in the restaurant, their table occupying the central room, and outside, dozens of Japanese paparazzi and eager fans gawped through the window, trying to get a glimpse of the world-famous supermodel and her boyfriend. The group was used to the media circus that followed them around. They almost didn't pay attention to it anymore. The desperate clamor for an exclusive photograph, as if the photographers themselves needed the once-in-a-lifetime images more than the air they breathed, was just a part of the job. Open the door in the morning, there was a photographer. Pull the drapes; there was another photographer. Take the trash out, guess what? Yet another photographer.

"I can't believe the show ran over by three hours," James said, chewing on a tempura shrimp. "How does that even work? Don't these venues have a schedule they need to keep to?"

"Something like that would never happen in the U.S.," Tom said, digging into his plate of custom-ordered chicken nuggets and french fries. "These people are just disorganized. Period."

"Oh, come on, Tom," Sarah replied. "Don't you remember Cincinnati, 2021? That show ran so late the cops came and shut it down before Elena even made it onto the catwalk."

"They still paid up, though," Max added, taking another sushi roll. "There was no way I was letting them get out of that one."

"Capitalism in all its glory, people," Samantha replied, rolling her eyes. "Hey, this is a nice place, though."

The restaurant was almost completely encased within huge tropical fish tanks filled with the most exotic sea life from Japan's varied coastline, including blue neon gobies, crystal red shrimp, tosakin goldfish, rotund pufferfish, and bright pink spider crabs. Lily sat there, watching as the bizarre creatures watched back from behind the glass as if she was the craziest-looking thing they had ever seen. She felt like she was in another world, on another planet, in another time. It was a whole universe away from Detroit and the cheap burger joints, seedy bars, and criminal hangouts of her old neighborhood.

Elena spotted her staring. "Making you think of home?" she asked.

"It's reminding me how much I don't miss the place," Lily replied.

"Hey, it had it's good points."

"Not like this."

"This is just fiction, you know that, right? This isn't real."

"Seems real enough to me."

"Oh, the illusion is real, but it's all temporary. Nothing here is permanent. Blink, and it will all be gone."

"Why would you say that? You thinking of quitting?"

Elena sipped an Espresso Martini and dabbed at her lipstick. "Maybe. Maybe not. It's just that sometimes I feel everything has happened so quickly, and my life is racing away from me faster than a bullet, you know?"

"It's a pretty good life, though, Elena. If it is racing away, you just need to keep up."

"Maybe I can't."

"Maybe you have to. Look around you. Look at how many people are relying on what you do. If you stop, everybody here has to find somebody else to hang onto."

"Maybe that's what they need. I'm not a golden goose, Lily. I'm just a kid from Detroit who wears clothes for a living. I don't cure people of terrible diseases or help children who are dying of starvation. I'm just a celebrity who's having her moment in the spotlight. Eventually, that light will burn out, and we'll just be left in the darkness, wondering what the hell just happened."

"You're getting deep, Elena. We're just in Tokyo, remember? We're killing time until our flight tomorrow. Maybe you should just enjoy the moment and go back to doing what you do best."

"Enjoy what?" James asked, brushing past Lily, his hand lingering a moment longer than necessary on her shoulder. "Enjoy the booze? Hell, why not? Another drink, Elena, my lovely?"

"I'll come with you," Elena said, standing and shooting her friend a wry smile. "I want to know what magic ingredient they're slipping into my glass."

Present Time – Churchill, Canada

Emily printed the report and headed back toward the main lodge. She had to find a way to get the information to Ethan without alerting the others. They had all been duped by the killer until now, but the murderer had made a mistake, and drugging the photographer had been a big one. They had obviously acted out of sheer panic, which was surprising because, until now, they had been so controlled. The toxicology report was as conclusive as it could get—there was no denying the evidence. The killer had told her they had the drug with them just two days ago, but the information had barely registered with her. Now, it screamed out at her like a dramatic news headline. Emily now knew who drugged Tom Oates, and that meant she knew who the killer was. However, she knew it would be a mistake to reveal her hand before she and her partner had a moment to regroup. They'd been outsmarted every step of the way and now was not the time to be hasty. The pair of them were used to being in front of things when it came to cracking cases, but in this case, they'd been two steps behind ever since they'd set foot on that plane.

She stepped out onto the walkway, which was now waist-deep in snow. She groaned, grabbed a snow shovel from inside the lab, and started digging. It was hard work, and it was taking up time she didn't have. Every minute lost was a minute the killer gained. Time to figure out a way to talk themselves out of the mess they had to know they were in. That was dangerous. Killers who backed themselves into a corner usually came out fighting.

She kept digging, knowing that Ethan was in there, unaware of what she'd found. She paused for a moment, realizing that she was being dumb. She could just call him.

She dropped the shovel and stepped back into the lab with her phone in her hand. She swiftly located his number and hit dial. It rang, but there was no answer. That was unlike Ethan. Usually, he answered right away. She glared at the phone. She didn't know what to make of it. Had something happened inside the lodge? Had the killer revealed themselves? It was frustrating. Ethan was just thirty feet away, but he may as well have been on the other side of the world.

She glared at the haphazard attempt she'd made at clearing a path before remembering she had another means of communication. The radio. She'd handed her partner one when he'd insisted on chasing after the Air Marshal. Her walkie was lying on the table beside Elena's body. She ran to it and picked it up. Something told her Ethan was in trouble, and that meant she had to get a message to him. She raised the radio to her lips and spoke.

***

"Ethan, it's me, Emily, over."

"Ethan, come on, pick up. Over."

"This is really urgent. Whatever you're doing, stop doing it and answer the radio. Over."

"Ethan, do you hear me? Tell me, you hear me?"

"Ethan! Answer the goddamn radio!"

Ethan rolled onto his side and forced his eyes open. He could barely see. The room was just a mash of dim lights and swirling shadows. What was that noise? Was somebody talking to him? It sounded like Emily, but he couldn't see her. Was she in the room?

Somebody had taken his phone, and he suspected he knew who it was. It had to be the person Sarah Locke had told Harper Mayfield about. Elena Hart's killer.

"Ethan, please. I need to talk to you. You're in danger."

Emily's voice was thin and raspy, as if she was suffering from a heavy cold, but he knew that wasn't what it was at all. It was an electronic sound, something Ethan had heard before but couldn't place like a transistor radio. He tried to turn his head toward the noise, but every movement was like a hammer slamming into his skull. It felt like somebody had kicked him in the head.

He saw the blood on the floor. It clung to his face like syrup. Whoever had cracked him across the skull had hit him pretty hard, but not hard enough to kill him. That could prove to be their biggest mistake.

There was something on the floor, and he realized it must have slipped from his belt when he'd collapsed. He could barely make it out, but he knew what it was. The radio that Emily had handed him earlier in the day. It was just lying there in his blood. He tried to reach out, but his arm felt like lead, so he slithered toward it, trying to kick out with his jelly legs, his body moving across the linoleum like a gigantic worm. Gradually, his body started to come around.

"Ung," he said, his tongue like a ball of cotton in his mouth. "Ung coman."

He was so close now, not more than three feet away. He continued pushing with his dead legs, watching the black shadow grow closer as his face slid against the linoleum.

"Ethan, please pick up," Emily said, "please, I need you to answer me." Her voice had lost all its usual energy.

Don't give up on me, Em, he thought. *Don't hang up. I'm almost there. I swear to you, I'm almost there.*

He was upon it now, his forehead nudging the electronic device, pushing it toward the wall. He needed to press the intercom, but he didn't know if his hands would comply. He tried to move his right arm, but it was trapped beneath him, so he used his left. It moved slowly at first, his fingers like claws, grasping at air as if it could propel his hand toward the radio. His index finger touched the smooth plastic, and then his thumb moved closer, and suddenly, the radio was within his elastic grasp. He reached for the intercom as he slowly raised himself to a sitting position. His head was still screaming out at him, but he was regaining the movement in his arms and legs.

"Em, it's me," he said as his voice slowly came back to life.

"Ethan, oh, thank goodness. I thought something had happened to you."

"It kinda did. Somebody cracked me over the head."

"Are you okay?"

"I've had worse. I just need to sit here for a minute while my head clears. Where are you?"

"I'm on the walkway between the lodge and the lab, but it's completely snowed in. I'm going to dig it out, but I wanted to tell you the results of the test as soon as possible."

"Go on."

"You're not going to believe this."

He thought about what Harper had said over the phone. With any luck, what Emily was about to tell him matched what Sarah Locke had revealed. "I think I might."

"It's about the contents of the cup. It wasn't just filled with water. There were two other substances in there, both of which one of the passengers specifically told me they had in their possession when I spoke to them two days ago."

"Go on."

"OK, but if anyone hands you a drink, don't take it. The killer drugged Tom Oates with a powerful concoction of liquid Valium and vodka. Ethan, do you know who told me she carried that with her wherever she went?"

Ethan didn't, but he was hoping the answer matched what he thought he knew.

"We've been chasing the wrong person all along," Emily said. "The killer isn't Max Roth, Tom Oates, or Michael Rodriguez at all. It's..."

One Year Before – Tokyo, Japan

The idea didn't come to her right away. It wasn't like she hated Elena. She loved her. They'd worked together for such a long time they were almost like family. She liked her job, too, even though it was stressful and she was away from home for most of the year. That was okay with her. She'd wanted this lifestyle anyway. She'd wanted what Elena had, but only the world didn't see her that way. Her looks were too conventional, too easy to forget. Elena's were unique in a 'girl from the streets come good' kind of way. Her nose wasn't completely straight, and her chin was a little pointy, but this was the twenty-first century, and modeling agencies didn't want 'easy on the eye' anymore. They wanted 'smack me in the face with personality, and 'give me something I haven't seen before.' Couple that with Elena's charm and easygoing personality, and all of a sudden, every glossy magazine this side of the eastern block wanted her on their front cover. It wasn't fair, it wasn't right, but that was the reality of it. She'd had to play second fiddle, and while that had been okay at first, this little extended trip to Tokyo had shown her a side of life she didn't want to let go of. The glamor, the opulence, the downright carefree way in which money was being thrown around. She wanted some of that. In fact, she wanted all of it.

The way the boyfriend's hand had caressed her shoulder hadn't gone unnoticed either. He liked her; that much was obvious. Sure, he was Elena's, but how many men had her boss slept with since they'd been friends, and not one of them had lasted the distance. This one was no exception. He was fake, he was hiding something, and that made him so much more interesting. Loyal men were boring. She longed for some intrigue and drama. Something to keep her awake at night. Something that would make her mind race. Nothing could be more dramatic than sleeping with James Bateman behind Elena Hart's back. It was a news story waiting for a headline.

She lay there in bed, thinking about those damn fish. There was something about them. The colors, the shapes, the way they kept looking at her, as if they wanted to tell her something important but didn't know how. It was the pufferfish that stood out the most with its slowly expanding body and thorny skin. She couldn't figure out why, but then she remembered something she'd read in a magazine when she was a kid, and suddenly, a plan began to form in her mind. Maybe there were other ways of getting what she wanted without hanging around the industry, clinging onto Elena's coattails while waiting for somebody to notice her.

Maybe Elena was the problem. Maybe with Elena out of the picture, the way ahead would be clear, and maybe, just maybe, Max Roth could find her the kind of modeling shoots she deserved. The more she thought about it, the more convinced she became, and the more the image of that bloated pufferfish kept coming back to her. She just needed someone who knew what he was doing and a little money to help her grease some palms.

***

The next day, she went to Elena for a loan, explaining that the extended trip to Tokyo had left her a little short. She knew Elena would oblige. She always did. As much as she hated standing in her shadow, the table scraps were always worth waiting for. When she got back to her room, she made a call. She had a friend who worked for a Tokyo private investigations agency who was willing to pass on information for a few thousand yen. After she'd wired the money, he told her there was a guy near Kiyosumi Garden who had the expertise she was looking for. Their flight wasn't until later that evening, so she had time to catch the metro, meet with the guy, and get back in time.

The building across from the garden was shabby, to say the least, but she was determined to go through with her plan. It had now become so much more than a crazy notion in her head. It was something she just had to do. She'd convinced herself it was what her life needed, the jolt of electricity that would springboard her to bigger and better things. Why should Elena have everything she couldn't? Why should Elena be the lucky one when she worked half as hard? Sure, what she was planning for Elena was a felony that carried a life sentence, but she didn't plan on being caught. In fact, she planned on pinning it on somebody else.

She tapped on the door of the apartment, expecting someone in a lab coat to answer, but instead, it was a young guy in a black tee and black jeans. His hair hung in front of his eyes as he looked up at her.

"You want toxin?"

"I do," she replied. "Can you help?"

"You have the money?"

She reached into her bag, revealing the bundles of yen.

"Come inside."

A part of her told her to run, but the other part told her to suck it up—nothing in this life was free, and good things didn't come easy. She followed the guy into the dingy apartment and turned into a room that glowed with an intense blue and sang with a repetitive hum. Inside were rows and rows of glass tanks, and inside those tanks were dozens of puffer fish.

"You have a lot of fish," she said.

"Need lots of fish to get what you need, lady."

He reached into a refrigerator and extracted a vial filled with a murky liquid.

"And this will do the job? Shouldn't I have more?"

"More will cost you double? You want more?"

She eyed her bag. She had barely enough for the one vial. "No, this is fine. And I just inject it into the...subject?"

"Stab with syringe and the pufferfish will do their job," he said. "It's not complicated. You want to kill? This will kill."

She handed over the money, took the vial, and got out of there as fast as she could. She had what she needed. Now, all she had to do was go through with it.

She arrived back at the hotel later than expected, and when she turned toward the door, she ran headlong into Sarah Locke. Her bag slipped from her shoulder, and all its contents spilled onto the floor.

"Oh, I'm so sorry," Sarah said. "I didn't see you."

"It's okay, it's not a problem."

She scurried across the sidewalk, trying to grab her purse, her lipstick, her...

"Is this yours?"

She looked up to see Sarah standing there with the vial nestled in her palm.

"Yes. Thanks."

Sarah's eyes narrowed. "Are you in some kind of trouble?"

"Trouble? No. Why would you think that?"

"Because this looks like some serious shit to me."

She was at a loss for words, floundering for the right thing to say.

"I've just been having a hard time keeping up with Elena's schedule," she said. "I needed something to pick me up, you know? Give me some energy?"

"So what is it?" Sarah asked, moving closer and lowering her voice. "Heroin?"

"No, nothing like that. Just a little herbal remedy I bought from some Japanese guy."

"So it's legal?"

She nodded. "Kinda. It's not dangerous if that's what you're thinking."

Before Sarah had a chance to object, Elena emerged with James on her arm, and the limousine pulled up out front. That was the only time she and Sarah Locke spoke about the vial of tetrodotoxin she'd acquired from a side street in Tokyo and the only time she looked at it again until she stepped onto that plane.

***

It took her almost a year to work up the courage to go through with her plan. In that time, she and James Bateman had started seeing each other. They were casual at first, illicit hookups that almost always ended up with them in bed. The sex was fun, but it wasn't the real reason she wanted the guy. It was who he was dating that was important to her. As the weeks and months blurred into one, and they went on photo shoot after photo shoot, the thrill of it started to wane, but she just couldn't stop. It was as though if she took her foot off the pedal, her journey to fame and wealth would become derailed. James was her link to a life she wanted so badly, and that link was precious to her.

She almost brought him in on her plan, but she didn't think she could trust him. Elena was his golden ticket, and he wasn't about to give her up lightly. That was when she had the idea to recruit the ex-soldier with the Elena Hart obsession. He seemed too perfect. Another friend she knew from school had bunked with the guy during his time in the military and had told her all about the photographs on Rodriguez's wall. When she'd learned he was now an Air Marshal, she opened up the lines of communication via an anonymous chat site, told Rodriguez about Elena's planned shoot in Churchill, and before she knew it, Rodriguez had hooked up with Sarah Locke and wormed his way onto the trip. The whole thing had worked out too perfectly. She was convinced that something was going to go wrong to throw the whole thing off, but little by little, the day of the flight grew closer, and she became more and more confident it was going to work.

***

When she stepped onto the Gulfstream, she was taken aback. The cabins were smaller than she'd anticipated, and she hadn't expected the whole entourage to fly with them. It meant she was going to have to wait for her moment.

She'd taken a seat near Elena, knowing she liked to slip a couple of Valium before takeoff to settle her nerves and hoping the right opportunity presented itself. She expected the Air Marshal to sit up front, but she hadn't expected the Neanderthal photographer to be there, too.

She also hadn't expected James to make a play for her so blatantly during the flight. While Elena lay there sleeping, he followed her to the bathroom.

"So, you wanna join the mile-high club or what?" he'd said.

"Are you kidding? Elena's right over there."

"Oh, she's so out of it, she'll never hear a thing."

"Maybe not, but somebody else might catch on."

"You think they don't know? Everybody knows, but don't worry. They're too scared of Elena to risk upsetting her. Our secret's safe."

"I don't care; I'm not doing anything on this plane."

He grabbed her ass and squeezed. "Oh, come on. Live a little."

"Get your damn hands off me." She pushed him away, causing Tom to look up from his paperback.

"Everything okay over there?" he asked.

"Yes, fine," she said. "We were just arguing over who gets to use the bathroom first."

"I thought you liked the excitement," James whispered. "I thought this was what you wanted."

"It was, but maybe it's been going on too long."

"What are you saying?"

She thought about the vial in her handbag and the plan she was about to go through with. She didn't need James anymore. She didn't need anything that was going to prevent her from fulfilling her destiny. "I'm saying it's over."

**

Later in the flight, when everybody retired to the rear cabin to play poker, she watched and waited. Elena was sleeping just behind the photographer and across from the Air Marshal. She knew she was going to have to play it very carefully. When Rodriguez headed toward the bathroom, she knew it was now or never. Once she heard the click of the door locking, she headed toward the front cabin.

"Where are you going, little lady?" Leo cried, putting on his best cowboy accent.

"Well, if you all are going to insist on taking my money," she replied in a voice that was half Calamity Jane, half Jessie from Toy Story, "then I'm going to have to get me some more cash."

As the others laughed, she headed toward Elena's seat, withdrew the syringe from her purse, and held her breath. This was it. This was the moment she'd been waiting for. If she didn't do it now, she never would. She eyed the photographer. His head was buried in his book, and he was unaware of her presence. She glanced at the bathroom door, which was firmly shut, but she knew Rodriguez would be back shortly. She chanced a peek over her shoulder, but everyone, including James Bateman, who had been sulking ever since their bathroom breakup, was focused on the game.

She looked down at Elena. She didn't deserve this, but in a game where only one player could win, her best friend had to be the loser. That was just the way things were. She held the syringe to the base of her neck and pushed. Elena didn't even flinch. She let the liquid flow into her body, making sure it was all deposited before withdrawing the needle and slipping it back into her purse. She had a place to hide it when the time was right. She let out a long breath. She'd done it. She was now a criminal. The thought excited her.

There was the whoosh of a toilet flushing and the click of a deadbolt being retracted, but it didn't matter. Lily was already back at the poker table, placing her bet and knowing that whatever happened, she was a winner.

Chapter 13

Into the White

The moment Emily knew she had been sucker punched was when she'd managed to dig through the snow, stepped into the relative warmth of the lodge, and was grabbed from behind. She felt the cold steel of the gun to her head as her attacker pulled their arm across her throat. She could smell the vodka on her breath and sense the adrenaline coursing through her veins.

"Lily," Emily said. "You don't need to do this."

"On that point, we'll have to disagree," Lily said, putting Emily's body between herself and Ethan as he stepped out of the office. Emily could see the dried blood on Ethan's head and the long line of it down his neck.

"I see you took my gun," Ethan said.

"It was the obvious play."

"You really want to kill a police officer?" Emily asked. "On top of what you've already done."

"Way I see it, things can't get much worse."

"Oh, but they can," Ethan countered. "You confess to Elena Hart's murder, and maybe the judge will look a little more favorably on you. You kill somebody else, you're a serial killer, and those people don't get released early."

"It was you?" James said, standing. "You killed Elena?"

"Oh, sit down," Lily hissed. "Don't try to convince me you hadn't thought about it, too. You were the one who tried to convince her to add you to the will. We all knew what you were up to. You conned your way into her life, conned your way into my bed, and if you'd had the balls, you would have killed her for the money."

"No way," James replied. "I'm not a murderer."

"No, you're nothing, James. You were nothing to me, and you were nothing to Elena. You weren't even the guy you pretended to be. If she'd have still been alive, you'd have lasted a few more weeks. Maybe less."

"You bitch," Max interjected. "Elena was a wonderful human being."

"Give me a break," Lily said. "You were taking her for everything she had. Without Elena, you would still be working the clubs, barely making enough to get by. Elena was your meal ticket, but that wasn't enough for you. Elena's biggest flaw was she didn't see through you until it was too late."

"You have no idea about the relationship Elena and I had."

"I know enough. I know that she'd already put a new agent on standby, and I also know about the two hookers and the bag of coke you were caught with. You're the same as James. You didn't care about Elena. You cared about the lifestyle."

"And what about Tom?" Ethan said. "Why get the photographer out of the picture."

Lily laughed. "It was my mistake, really. When he took me hostage, I really thought he was going to kill me. I told him I was about to come into some real money from a new deal I was working. I said I'd give him a cut if he let me go. He asked me what it was, and I told him that I'd done something I wasn't proud of but that, as a result, I now had the potential to become a very wealthy woman."

"And Tom put two and two together."

"He didn't say as much, but I could see it in his eyes. When he said he wanted to talk to you, Detective, I knew I couldn't take any chances."

"So you laced his drink with Valium and vodka," Emily said. "A dangerous concoction that could render the recipient unconscious pretty quickly. You told me you had the Valium but not the vodka."

"I'm a pretty good poker player," Lily said, smirking. "I rarely declare my entire hand. I knew Tom wouldn't react to finding vodka in his cup. The guy was a big drinker. He probably saw it as a good thing."

"And then you snuck into the office and hit me over the head," Ethan said, leaning against the wall to steady himself.

"I snuck a wrench from one of the shelves in the backroom. I wanted you out of action for a while. I can see now I should have hit you harder."

"But why did you do it?" Emily asked, trying to keep her assailant talking.

"You wouldn't understand."

"Try me."

"Being a woman in the modeling industry is hard. It's so hard. It's all I ever wanted to be. Ever since I was a little girl. My mom pushed me into beauty pageants, and we traveled all over the country. She laughed. "Can you believe I was Little Miss Michigan in 2007? My mom used to tell me it was the proudest moment of her life, seeing her little eleven-year-old daughter lifting that crown. I just remember being terrified of the judges, but something about it stuck with me. It became an addiction. I was the hottest thing on the kid's circuit for a few years. Elena was nowhere to be seen back then. I was the queen of Detroit, not her. *Me.*"

"But something changed," Emily said. "Something happened?"

"I hit puberty," Lily hissed. "My body changed, my face changed. Suddenly, I wasn't the judges' favorite anymore. Other people started to overtake me. I slipped down the ranking, dropping out of the top ten and then out of the top twenty. My own mother started to lose faith in me, telling me perhaps I should consider cosmetic surgery as if I was suddenly ugly. I'm not ugly; everybody can see that. I just lost whatever it is the industry wanted at that time."

"Then you met Elena?"

"Right. Then I met Elena, the teenager who people really were talking about. She beat me into first place at a pageant in Chicago, which really pissed me off, but my mom, she seemed to really enjoy it. I don't know; maybe she saw something in Elena that she no longer saw in me."

"So, you became jealous?"

"I'm not a jealous person, not usually, but yeah. Your mom tells you somebody else is more beautiful than you? That kinda hurts. Anyway, my mom urged me to go talk with her, so I did, you know? Back when I was young, I just did what my mom asked, and that was when Elena and I became friends, but more than that. We became sisters because my mom really looked at Elena like she was another daughter.

"Elena would be round all the time, and my mom would coach her on what to wear, how to look, how to hold herself. She stopped telling me those kind of things because I think by then she suspected I didn't have what it took, and Elena did. I started doing Elena's makeup around that time just to get some praise from my mom. She liked the way I did it, and so when Elena started landing bigger and bigger shows, Elena felt obliged to keep me on.

"Little by little, Elena forgot about my mom, and when she got cancer, Elena never came to see her. I never let on to Elena, but I've never forgiven her for that. Mom was the reason her career took off, but Elena never mentioned her name in interviews and never gave her the credit she deserved.

"I told Elena I was late for the flight because my mom had had a bad spell, and that was only partially a lie. My mom's been having bad spells for months, but Elena never asked about her, and she never noticed the change in me. Do you know, even though my mom is on her deathbed, whenever I'm there, she asks how Elena's doing? Not how I'm doing. How Elena's doing."

Emily could feel Lily stiffen as she spoke, as if the memory was so painful for to recall, her body was literally fighting against it.

"Anyway," she continued, "before I knew it, I was no longer modeling. I was just a makeup artist who'd had no training in her profession. I felt like a fraud as if I was caught between the life I wanted and being back out on the streets. Doing makeup kept me in the industry and around the right people, so I thought I'd do it for a while until the industry changed and my modeling career would kick off again, but I was so busy with Elena's career that I kind of forgot about my own. That was until a weekend in Tokyo when everything became clear to me again."

"And that was where you discovered Tetrodotoxin," Ethan said, "which is what Sarah Locke remembered seeing you with after she came to. She says she ran into you at the Ritz-Carlton, Tokyo, and you had a vial of murky liquid in your bag. That was Tetrodotoxin, wasn't it?"

"I knew that bitch would remember our little encounter one day," Lily said. "I just knew it. I thought about killing her, too, but that would have been too obvious. Sarah and I, we never really got on."

"The only thing I can't figure out," Ethan said, "is what you did with the syringe. We had the team scour every inch of that airplane, including the runway. They found nothing."

Lily pulled her arm tightly across Emily's throat while tucking the gun in her waistband. She then slid a hidden compartment from the heel of her shoe and plucked the murder weapon from within, holding it up so that the light glistened off its sharp tip. "I guess I thought of everything, Detective."

"So what did you think would happen after you got away with Elena's murder," Emily asked, choosing not to seize the opportunity her captor had presented to her in order to uncover the truth. "What did you stand to gain from killing her."

"Revenge for the way she stole my career?" Lily said. "Maybe a feeling that I'd paid something back? But most of all, I really believed that with Elena out of the way, I could focus on my career again, and maybe I could take over where Elena left off. Maybe I could convince Max to get me some of the assignments Elena could no longer fulfill."

"You have to be kidding me," Max spat. "You? You don't have it, Lily. Never have. Elena was worth a thousand of you. A million."

Lily pushed Emily aside before retrieving the gun and pointing it at Max.

"Oh, is that so?" she cried. "Is that why you were constantly telling me how one day you and I should do something on the side? That maybe Elena wasn't as good as she thought she was and that maybe I could take her place."

"Yes...yes, and I meant it," Max said, holding out his hands. "Please, don't shoot."

"Look at you, you sniveling weasel. You're full of bravado when you're the one holding the cards. You're always the first to give a pretty woman a compliment or grab a model by the ass when she's just trying to squeeze past. But when I'm the one holding the gun, suddenly you're the one cowering in the corner."

She fired over Max's shoulder, blasting a chunk out of the wall.

"Woah!" he cried. "Lily, please, don't do this."

"And what about you, James," she said, turning the gun on him. "Or is it Aaron? I get confused. You told me you loved me, even though you were still sleeping with Elena. Which was it?"

"Of course I love you," he replied, the charm returning to his eyes. "I always loved you, Lily. It was always you. Not Elena."

"Bullshit!" she yelled, shooting into the ceiling, causing James to back away with his hands held up.

"You're all evil!" she hollered. "All of you. James, Max, Tom, even Samantha, and Leo. You were constantly on Elena's back for money. Not one of you loved Elena as I did. Not one of you cared about her. This is on you as much as it's on me. Elena was just a means to an end for every single one of you. A bank you could all withdraw money from whenever you wanted. Now, what are you going to do, people? Where are you going to get your designer clothes, fast cars, and luxury hotels?"

Emily watched as Lily waved the gun around. She was clearly drunk, and that made her even more dangerous. If they were going to stop this before somebody got hurt, they were going to have to move fast. She eyed Ethan, who was edging closer, and that was when she knew he was going to make a move.

***

As soon as Emily was released, Ethan made a decision. He was taking Lily down, even though his legs still felt like rubber, the wound in his calf was screaming in pain, and his head was swimming. It didn't matter. This was what he was trained for.

It was the look that his partner gave him that signaled this was the time. Lily was behaving erratically, and if he didn't do something, at least one of them was going to get killed. When she shot at Max and then fired into the ceiling, he was left with no choice. She was trigger-happy and hellbent on violence.

When Lily stepped toward the others, he launched himself at her, reaching for the gun just as she squeezed the trigger. The bullet whistled past Samantha Mitchel's right shoulder and punctured a hole in the wall as he and Lily went tumbling to the floor. She was a lot stronger than she looked. He tried to pull the gun from her hands, but her grip was like a vice. The gun went off again, this time smashing the window, letting in the snow and cold air.

Emily moved next, pressing her knee into Lily's abdomen, pinning her to the floor, while Ethan held her arms. He shook her hand, dislodging the gun from her grip, and it went spinning across the floor.

"It's over, Lily," he said, watching as she writhed and kicked beneath him. "Lily Craven, I'm placing you under arrest for the murder of Elena Hart, two counts of assault—including one on a police officer—and the unlawful discharging of a firearm."

As he read her her rights, Lily just glared at the ceiling, no longer listening to him or anybody else in the room. He suspected she was thinking about the life she could have had if her plan had worked out and the glamorous existence that Elena Hart had enjoyed right up to the moment she had been killed. The whole thing was just one big tragedy with no winners. Just a lot of hurt and a bunch of regrets.

As Emily led her to one of the unoccupied rooms, Ethan considered what they'd all been through. Elena Hart's murder, the interviews in the police training lodge, the constant leaks to the press, the blizzard that had snowed them in, the endless revelations, the polar bear attack on Sarah Locke, the chase through the snow, the photographer's abduction of Lily Craven, and the Air Marshal shooting him in the leg. It had been a roller coaster of a few days, and one that was going to take a while to recover from, but even though they'd been through so much emotional and physical trauma, they'd eventually gotten to the bottom of who killed Elena Hart. That had to mean something. He knew it meant something to him, and it meant something to Emily. Deep down, he also knew it would have meant something to Rebecca.

It was what they were paid to do, after all. They were Detective Ethan Steele and Dr. Emily Carter from the Canadian Specialist Investigations Unit, and they never let the bad guys get away.

***

Ethan and Emily sat in the Churchill police headquarters, watching as the snow gradually abated outside. Lily Craven had been flown back to the US along with Tom Oates and Michael Rodriguez, both of whom would also be spending time in jail. In Lily's case, however, her stay would be much longer. Sarah Locke was still in the hospital but on the road to recovery, and Harper Mayfield was already back to her old ways, bugging Ethan for the exclusive she claimed he'd promised her.

Elena Hart had finally made it back home, where her parents were handling things. It felt poetic that she was back in Detroit after so many years on the road, doing what other people wanted her to do. Perhaps now she could finally be at peace.

Ethan had spent a night in the hospital, receiving treatment for his bullet wound and the lingering effects of concussion, but he hadn't stayed any longer than he had to. There were reports to be filed, questions to be answered, and bosses to keep happy.

"You know, I thought you were a goner back there," Emily said. "When I realized that Lily was the killer and, I couldn't get back to warn you."

"I thought the same of you," Ethan replied, noticing the slight bruising on Emily's temple where the gun had been pressed. "I knew Lily was so out of it; she was capable of anything."

"Would you have missed me?"

"I'd have to think about that," he joked. "I mean, you're always on at me all the time."

"Hey, that's not fair. If it wasn't for me, you'd never crack any cases."

"Yeah, I guess that's true. But if it wasn't for me, your life would be boring."

She laughed. He liked her laugh. It reminded him of a happier time when things in his life were more stable. Ever since Rebecca's death, he'd felt like he was on some sort of mission, but he didn't know where to. He wanted justice for his fiancée, but more than that, he wanted to stop what happened to Rebecca from happening to anybody else. If bringing Lily Craven to justice was a part of that, then so be it, but he knew there were so many more out there, so many people suffering because of selfish acts like those committed by Elena Hart's pretend best friend. If this was his mission, then it had only just begun.

"Are you looking forward to going home?" Emily asked him.

"I think so. Yeah."

"Do you have anything planned?"

"Drink myself into a stupor? Eat my body weight in pizza?"

Emily laughed again.

"No, I don't," he said eventually. "I don't really have anybody to go home to."

His words seemed to upset her. He hadn't meant them to. She touched his hand. "You're not alone, Ethan. You have friends. Friends like me."

"Is that what you are?"

"I think so. Do you?"

Ethan thought about that. Sure, he saw Emily as a co-worker, but she was a friend, too. They'd been working together so closely for such a long time that there was no way their relationship could be purely professional. He saw Emily more than any other woman in his life, and that had to mean something. Sometimes, he felt guilty. Guilty that he felt something for another woman. Guilty that they shared coffee together, ate together, and laughed at the same jokes. Guilty that he didn't miss Rebecca enough or that he didn't think of her every second. Guilty that he was still alive and Rebecca was in the ground. Guilty that her killer still walked free, and rather than being out there attempting to put him behind bars, he was sitting in a police station in Churchill, trying to decide whether his partner was his friend or whether she was so much more.

"I think we work well together," he said eventually, taking the easy option. Something flickered in her eyes. Disappointment? Confusion?

"What time are we flying out of here?" she asked, seemingly too embarrassed to look him squarely in the eyes.

"My flight's at six. I think yours is at—"

"Seven. Yes, that's right."

"We can get some dinner before we leave," he added, trying to mend a wound he suspected he'd created. "Maybe head down to the Dancing Bear. I hear they make a mean pizza."

"Maybe. If we get these reports done."

There was a silence between them that spoke louder than any words. He didn't know whether to break it or let it hang. Either way, they both knew what it meant. There was too much at stake for them to destroy what they had. They were both in a state of emotional trauma, multiplied by the near-death experience they had both shared. Now was not the time to act irrationally. Now was the moment for restraint.

His phone beeped, breaking the tension.

"Ethan Steele...hi Chief, what's up?...Okay, what are the details?... right, I see...and you say there are two bodies less than a mile apart... alright...and who's on the scene right now...local PD?...is the scene sealed off to the public?...Okay...got it...we're just wrapping up here, but flights permitting, I'd say we could be with them by tonight...sure, we'll certainly do our best...got it...I'll call you back when we're at the scene."

Emily had been watching his every move. "Sounded important."

"Double homicide. Newfoundland. Looks like the killer cut off their hands."

"Sounds nasty."

"Political, too."

"How so?"

"One of the victims was the mayor's son, the other, his political opponent's daughter."

"Holy crap."

"You said it."

Ethan grabbed his bag.

"Where are you going?" she asked.

"I'm grabbing us a cab to the airport."

Emily eyed the desk. "What about all these reports?"

"We can do it on the plane."

Emily stood and grabbed her coat. "Are you telling me we're going from one ice-covered location to another without even having the opportunity to go home to take a hot shower?"

Ethan smiled. "Would you have it any other way?"

Emily stood there with her arms folded, looking like the last thing she wanted to do was follow him to yet another crime scene where every suspect told them lies, and every witness had their own agenda, but slowly her frown began to shift, and a smile spread across her cheeks. It was right then he knew there was much more to come between them, and he couldn't wait to see where the journey would take them.

"I'll be right behind you, Steele," she said. "But this time, let's find a location we can actually leave."

Thank you for coming along on the journey as Detective Ethan Steele and Dr. Emily Carter brought justice to Elena Hart. Be sure to leave a review, tell me what you think, and tell other readers how much you enjoyed *Chill of Truth*

If you haven't had the chance check out my other book, *Gone Mia*

Where love can blind us to mortal danger...

Smalltown introvert Mia Agostini has long wondered if "the one" will ever find her. Then, one day, when her car breaks down, the handsome and handy Alex Bartlett comes to the rescue, offering more than a tire change. Mia is instantly smitten, and yet, what begins as a promising romance quickly takes a perilous turn.

Alex is teeming with dark secrets—and isn't anyone's savior.

Soon fleeing her home, Mia finds Alex in relentless pursuit, determined to prevent her escape. Trapped by a deep desire for love, one woman who's long been waiting for change must now step up and claim it.

Embracing her instincts will now be crucial. It's time for a total transformation—and a whole new game of deception...

Remember to check in with me, Tess Raynes for all my new releases.

Happy Reading!

Tess

www.ingramcontent.com/pod-product-compliance
Lightning Source LLC
Chambersburg PA
CBHW050449110726
47899CB00003B/868